At the age of eight **Michelle Douglas** was asked what she wanted to be when she grew up. She answered, 'A writer.' Years later she read an article about romance writing and thought, *Ooh, that'll be fun.* She was right. When she's not writing she can usually be found with her nose buried in a book. She is currently enrolled in an English Masters programme for the sole purpose of indulging her reading and writing habits further. She lives in a leafy suburb of Newcastle, on Australia's east coast, with her own romantic hero—husband Greg, who is the inspiration behind all her happy endings. Michelle would love you to visit her at her website: www.michelle-douglas.com

Books by Michelle Douglas:

BELLA'S IMPOSSIBLE BOSS
THE MAN WHO SAW HER BEAUTY
THE SECRETARY'S SECRET
CHRISTMAS AT CANDLEBARK FARM
THE CATTLEMAN, THE BABY AND ME

For Maggie, who is everything a sister should be.
Thank you!

If she pointed out to Cade that her title was in fact 'Nanny' and not 'Friend' or 'Family Member', it would give him the wrong impression. It would make it sound as if she didn't really care for Ella and Holly, and she did. She adored them.

It didn't change the fact that this was still a job, though, and that no matter how much Cade and his family welcomed her into their fold it still didn't make her one of them.

It wasn't anything to be bitter about. It wasn't anything to be hurt about. It was the truth—plain and simple.

Oh, but how she wished she had a family like his!

THE NANNY
WHO SAVED
CHRISTMAS

BY
MICHELLE DOUGLAS

First published in Great Britain 2012
by Mills & Boon, an imprint of Harlequin (UK) Limited.
Harlequin (UK) Limited, Eton House, 18-24 Paradise Road,
Richmond, Surrey TW9 1SR

© Michelle Douglas 2012

ISBN: 978 0 263 22831 1

Harlequin (UK) policy is to use papers that are natural, renewable and recyclable products and made from wood grown in sustainable forests. The logging and manufacturing process conform to the legal environmental regulations of the country of origin.

CHAPTER ONE

NICOLA craned to take in as much of the view as she could from the Cessna's window as they landed on an airstrip that was nothing more than red dirt, bordered here and there with spiky grass and mulga scrub. When the pilot cut the engine the sudden silence engulfed her.

He turned to her. 'Here we are then.'

'Right.' She swallowed and gave a curt nod. *Here* was the Waminda Downs cattle station in the far west of Queensland—the Outback, the Never-Never, beyond the Black Stump—and about as far from civilisation as a body could get. She glanced out of the window again and something in her chest started to lift. This place was the polar opposite to her native Melbourne. The *total* polar opposite.

'May I get out now?'

'Well, as this is your destination, love, I believe that's the plan.'

He let the steps down, she stuck her head outside and the first thing to hit her was the heat—hard, enveloping and intense. The second, when her feet found firm ground again, was the scent—hot, dry earth and sun-baked grasses. The lonely desolation thrust itself upon her consciousness with an insistence that refused to be ignored, greater than the heat that beat down on her uncovered head and greater than the alien sights and scents. A person could get lost out here and never be found.

She surveyed the endless expanse of pale brown grass, interspersed here and there with mulga scrub and salt-bush, and at all the red dirt beneath it, and for the first time in three months she felt like her heart started to beat at the right pace again. Out here she wouldn't encounter acquaintances who would glance at her and then just as quickly glance away again to whisper behind their hands. Or friends who would rush up to grip her hands and ask her how she was doing. Or those people who just plain enjoyed others' misfortunes and would smirk at her.

She closed her eyes and lifted her face to the sky. 'This is perfect.'

'Perfect for what?'

That voice didn't belong to Jerry the pilot.

Her eyes sprang open. She spun around to find a man hauling her suitcase from the plane's cargo hold. He set it on the ground and then straightened. He was tall and broad. He gave off an impression of strength. He gave off an even bigger impression of no-nonsense efficiency.

She blinked. 'Where did you come from?' So much for thinking she and the pilot were alone in this wilderness.

He pointed back behind him and in the harsh glare of the sun she caught the glint from a car's windscreen. 'You're from the station?'

One corner of his mouth hooked up. It wasn't precisely a smile, but she had a feeling it was meant to be friendly. 'I'm Cade Hindmarsh.'

Her boss.

He must be about thirty and he was tanned. Really tanned. He had deep lines fanning out from his eyes. Probably from all the habitual squinting into the sun one must do out here. A habit Nicola found herself mimicking already. He tipped his Akubra back from his head and she found herself staring into the bluest pair of eyes she'd ever seen. The sun might've faded everything else out here, but it hadn't faded them.

His gaze was direct. The longer she looked at him, the lighter she started to feel, a burden of weight slipping free from her shoulders and sinking into the dry earth at her feet. He didn't know her. He'd never met her before in his life. Nobody out here knew her. He wouldn't think her pitiful, stupid or a failure. Unless she did something to give him reason to.

She had absolutely no intention of letting that happen.

'Nicola McGillroy,' she said, recalling her manners and introducing herself. Cool, poised and businesslike, she lectured. That was the impression she wanted to give. And the antithesis of a pitiful doormat.

He strode over and extended his hand. She placed hers inside it and found it so comprehensively grasped it made her eyes widen. He grimaced and loosened his hold. 'Sorry. I'm always being told not to grip so hard.'

She swallowed. 'No need to apologise; you didn't hurt me.'

Cade shook hands the way she'd always thought men should shake hands. The reality, like so many other realities, had disappointed her. Cade didn't disappoint. His grip was firm, dependable. Strong. Men who shook hands like that didn't get pushed around. She wanted to learn to shake hands like that.

From beneath the brim of his Akubra those blue eyes twinkled for a moment. Her lips lifted in response, and then with a start she realised her hand was still held in his. She gently detached it.

Her employer tipped his head back and stared at her for several long, pulse-inducing moments. She lifted her chin and met his gaze square-on. She didn't kid herself that his survey was anything other than what it was—a sizing up…a summing up. For the next two months she would have charge of his two young daughters. She wouldn't respect any man who merely took her at face value, who went only by her résumé and a telephone interview. Even if that telephone interview had been gruelling.

'Will I do?' she finally asked, the suspense sawing on her nerves. She didn't doubt for one moment that if his answer was no he'd put her back on that plane and send her home to Melbourne.

The thought made her throat dry and her heart falter for a couple of beats before it surged against her ribs again with renewed force. She couldn't go back to Melbourne. Not yet!

Melbourne…December…with their joint reminders of the wedding she should've been planning. She didn't think she could stand it.

'Why is this place perfect?'

Perfect? Nicola Ann, you can't be serious!

Her mother's voice sounded in her head. Nicola resolutely ignored it. 'All of this—' she gestured to the landscape '—is so different to what I'm used to, but it's exactly what I imagined.'

'And that's good?'

'I think so.' It was *very* good.

He planted his feet. 'A lot of people who come out here are running away from something.'

She refused to let her chin drop. 'Is that why you're out here?'

Off to one side Jerry snorted, reminding her that she and her employer weren't alone. 'Love, generations of the Hindmarshes have been born and bred out here.'

She raised an eyebrow at Cade Hindmarsh. 'Is that a no, then?'

Those blue eyes twinkled again. 'That's a no.'

'Some people—' she chose her words carefully '—not only want to see what they can of the country, but to experience it as well.'

'And that's why you're here?'

'I know if you were born and bred out here that you're familiar with this kind of life and landscape, but being here is an adventure for me.' It was also a timeout from her real life, a much needed break from Melbourne with all its reminders of her short-sighted stupidity and her cringe-inducing ignorance. She didn't say that out loud though. He might interpret that as running away.

It will all still be here when you get home, you know, Nicola Ann.

And her mother might be right.

Though, in two months' time, hopefully she'd have found the strength to face it all again. She hoped that in two months' time she'd have changed, become a different person—someone stronger, tougher. Someone who didn't get taken advantage of, lied to or cheated on.

Finally Cade smiled. 'Welcome to Waminda Downs, Nicola.'

A pent-up breath whooshed out of her. 'Thank you.' She grinned. She couldn't help it. She wanted to high-five someone for having passed Cade's assessment. Jerry's chuckle told her that her excitement was visible for all to see.

Cade's smile broadened into a grin that made her blink and just like that she could practically feel Diane's elbow in her ribs and her whisper of, *Hot, gorgeous hunk* at her ear. The thought of her best friend pulled Nicola up short.

It made her pull back, compose her features and press her hands together at her waist.

Cade's eyes narrowed and his grin faded too until it had vanished completely. Something inside her protested at that, but she stamped it out. She was here to change. Not to gush. Not to be eager to approve of everything and everyone she met without considered judgement first. And not to be patted on the head and treated like a child.

She strode around him to seize her suitcase. 'I'm really looking forward to meeting Ella and Holly.'

Cade remained silent. Nicola bit her tongue to stop from prompting further. She wasn't here to make friends. She wasn't here to win approval—not from Cade, not from anyone. She was here to do a job…and to get her head screwed on straight again. She'd do both those things to the best of her ability.

'Brought that generator you ordered.'

The men unloaded the generator. Beneath his work shirt Cade's arm muscles bulged. Despite the generator's bulk and weight, he didn't so much as break out into a sweat as he carried it to the car. With a wave to Jerry, she set off after him, admiring the broad sweep of his shoulders and the depth of his chest. The man was a veritable Atlas. He stowed the generator into the tray of his ute with ease and then took her suitcase. She told herself the only reason she let him take it was because he'd know how to load the tray to best effect.

It wasn't because it was too heavy and she had pitiful upper body strength.

Her lip curled. Oh, who was she trying to kid? But getting fit was on her to-do list while she was out here. In two months' time she'd be tossing that suitcase around as if it weighed nothing at all. The way Cade did.

She found her eyes drawn too easily to him so, setting her teeth, she did what he did—shaded her eyes and watched as the Cessna took off. And then, to stop from staring at him again, she completed a slow three hundred and sixty degree turn to survey the landscape. Finally she shrugged. 'Okay, it beats me. The land looks flat for as far as the eye can see. At least until that ridge way over there.' She gestured to her right. 'But I can't see a homestead.'

'The land is deceptive.' He opened the car door for her, and his unwavering scrutiny made her clumsy. She knocked both an elbow and a knee as she climbed into her seat.

Oh, Nicola Ann, you are such a klutz.

He didn't say anything, but she swore those blue eyes of his twinkled before he closed the door.

Without another word he climbed into the driver's seat and they set off along what Nicola could only loosely describe as a track.

'Is it far to the homestead?'

'About five kilometres.'

She waited. He didn't say anything more. On the rough track the car couldn't go much faster than thirty kilometres an hour and the silence pressed in on her. Cade's tall, broad bulk dominated the interior cab and, for reasons she couldn't fathom, that made her nervous.

'Is the land near the homestead unsuitable for an airstrip?'

He flicked a glance in her direction. She doubted much got past those eyes of his. She could imagine them filling with that soul-destroying combination of derision and pity she'd seen in her friends' eyes during the last few months.

Yes, she could imagine it all too clearly and it made bile rise in her throat.

'Fire,' he said.

She blinked. 'I beg your pardon?'

'The reason the airstrip is away from the house is in case there's an accident that could start a bushfire.'

Oh. It made perfect sense when she thought about it.

At that moment they topped a rise and Cade pulled the car to a halt. She stared at the vista spread before her and her 'wow' breathed out of her before she could help it, before she could remind herself about tempering her enthusiasm and keeping things businesslike.

She shook herself and swallowed. 'Very impressive, Mr Hindmarsh.'

'Cade,' he corrected. 'We don't stand on ceremony out here, Nicola.' He gestured out of the front windscreen. 'As you can see, this is the station complex.'

It was much larger than anything she'd imagined. On the side nearest them was a sprawling homestead with two wings that spread out in a V shape from the main structure. The weatherboards were painted a crisp white and the corrugated iron roof a cool deep green. A veranda wrapped around it all, but it wasn't the homestead's size that stole her breath. It was the garden that surrounded it. Even from this distance she could make out the fronds of the two magnificent tree ferns that stood at the end of each wing, as well as the breadth of the date palms that dotted the lawn. 'I can't believe you have a garden. It's like an oasis.'

'Bore water,' he said. 'But I didn't stop here so you could admire the view. I need you to understand some basic facts so you can stay out of trouble while you're here.'

She frowned.

'You might think coming out here for two months is an adventure, but the land is unforgiving. Underestimate it at your own peril.'

She tried to suppress a shiver. 'Okay.' And then she realised how weak and pathetic her voice sounded. She lifted her chin and made her voice stronger. 'What do I need to know?'

'The land is deceptive to the eye. It undulates. You think you know where you are and then you turn around and can't see the homestead or any familiar landmarks. It's that easy—' he clicked his fingers '—to get lost. You're not to go wandering about on your own.'

Her heart sank. There went her plan of jogging her way to fitness and thinness.

Damn it! She'd sworn to return to Melbourne toned and tanned. It would signal to Diane, Brad and all her other friends that she was getting on with her life. It would prove that she had confidence and chutzpah and was no longer an object of pity. She gripped her hands together. And the next time a guy dumped her she wanted to make sure it wasn't because she was half a stone overweight.

'Waminda Downs covers three million acres. That's twelve thousand square kilometres.'

She pulled her mind back.

'That's a lot of ground to cover if someone goes missing.'

She read the subtext. If a person went missing out here they might never be found.

'See that perimeter fence? It's painted white.'

'Yes.'

'That encloses the four acres of the home paddock, including the homestead and outbuildings. You can wander freely within that, but do not cross that boundary unaccompanied.'

Four acres would be plenty! 'Roger.'

'And I'd like you and the girls to stay away from the cattle yards.' He pointed to a series of yards on the side furthest away from them. They were separated from the homestead by a number of outbuildings. He proceeded to name the buildings. 'That's the machinery shed.' It was huge. 'Barn and stables.' He pointed. 'Next to them is the jackaroo and jillaroo quarters. Those smaller cottages at the far end are for the stockmen and their families.'

She blinked. Waminda Downs, it seemed, was its own thriving community.

'Why are the cattle yards out of bounds?' She wanted to understand every hazard in her new environment so she could head off any potential disasters.

'We corralled a herd of brumby in there the week before last and we're going to start breaking them in. It's dangerous work.'

'Okay.' She nodded once, hard. 'Anything else I need to know?'

'If you do go exploring within the home paddock you always take a water bottle with you, and wear a hat and sunscreen. It's only four acres, but it's summer and at the height of the day the sun is merciless.'

'Don't worry, Mr Hindmarsh. I won't be letting the girls outside between eleven a.m. and three p.m.'

'The garden is surprisingly cool.'

She'd make her own judgement about that. Located two hours by plane from the nearest hospital, she had no intention of risking sunstroke in her charges.

'And there's just one final thing.'

Something in his tone made her turn. 'Yes?'

His blue eyes flashed. 'The name's Cade—try it.'

She'd never had a problem calling any of her previous employers by their first name, but it suddenly occurred to her that she didn't want to be on a first name basis with this man. She swallowed. He was too…too confident, too gorgeous…too *everything* that she wasn't. He brought home to her all the things she lacked with a realness that made her want to turn her face away.

Coward.

For heaven's sake, she was his children's nanny. First names could not be avoided. She lifted her chin. She would be cool and poised. She would be competent and clever. She would be respected. She moistened her lips. His eyes followed the action. 'Cade,' she said. His name scraped out of her throat with an appalling huskiness and none of the poised cool she'd tried so hard to carry off.

He cocked an eyebrow. 'See? Wasn't so hard, was it?'

Before she could answer he started the engine again and they set off towards the homestead. This time she curbed any impulse to fill the silence. She focused instead on the homestead and garden, and tried to make out what it was that glittered on the trunks of the date palms and to see what the shapes were that littered the lawn.

And as they drew closer her jaw started to drop. The glitter...it was tinsel. The shapes on the lawn...

Oh. My. God. The shapes were Christmas-themed wooden cut-outs painted in the brightest colours imaginable. On one side of the lawn a Santa sleigh squatted along with four merry reindeer. On the other stood a wooden Santa in all his holiday merriment, a sack of toys at his feet. Gold and silver snowflakes hung from the veranda ceiling, alternating with green and red stars. Tinsel in every colour twined around the veranda posts.

She flinched. *Christmas.* Oh, she'd known she wouldn't be able to avoid it completely—Cade had two young daughters after all—but...

She'd thought that out here in the Never-Never it'd be small-scale, low-key...restrained.

It hit her then that she'd been counting on it. Her chest cramped.

The car stopped at the edge of a path lined with oversized candy canes that she knew would light up at night.

At the end of the path four broad steps led to the veranda and the front door of the homestead. It was a testament to the door's solidity that it didn't buckle beneath the weight of its enormous wreath. Three wooden angels graced the roof of the veranda, their trumpets raised heavenward as if heralding the arrival of the silly season.

She bit her tongue to stop from blurting out something unpoised and stupid. Her hands fisted and she blinked hard to counter the stinging in her eyes. All this Christmas-ness was a too-vivid reminder of the merriment and festivity she'd known herself incapable of taking part in back home. It reminded her of the wedding she should've been planning. It taunted her with all she'd lost and how nothing— *nothing*—could ever replace it.

It was only the first week of December. She'd taken a month's leave from her job as a teacher and her four weeks of Christmas holidays, because Christmas and wedding preparations had become synonymous in her mind. But Christmas with all its gaudy festivity now stared her in the face. The joke was on her. She swallowed and tried to ignore the ache that spread through her chest.

'Now I'll warrant this isn't what you were expecting.'

Beside her, Cade chuckled. She couldn't open her mouth to either agree or disagree.

'What do you think?'

She hated it! The truth, though, would not endear her to him. Of that she was certain. And while she told herself she didn't give two hoots what her employer thought of her—other than that she did her job well—deliberate rudeness was not in her nature. Nor was it poised, elegant or dignified. She tried to think of something coolly elegant to say…or even something bland and inoffensive.

She turned to Cade, she racked her brain and then realised she needn't have bothered. One glance at his face told her he'd perceived her true feelings on the matter. His eyes narrowed and while there was no denying that he was broad, big and strong, for the first time he looked formidable too.

She swallowed. She couldn't find a smile, but she struggled for light. 'To think I'd left all this behind in the city.'

His lips tightened. 'So that's what you're running from.'

'I'm not running from anything.' Taking a timeout wasn't running.

He leaned back, but his eyes remained flint hard. Blue flint in a landscape of khaki and brown. The pulse in her throat swelled and pounded. 'That generator I just unloaded, it's to run all the coloured fairy lights I'm planning on hanging from the house and around the garden in the next week or two.'

The homestead would look like some tacky fairy tale palace. She sucked in a breath. Or an overdecorated wedding cake.

'We're doing Christmas big out here this year, Ms McGillroy. If that's going to be a problem for you then it's not too late for me to radio Jerry to come back and fly you out of here.'

So she could face all this insubstantial, bubble-popping, fake merriment in Melbourne? No, thank you very much! She could put on a happy face and *do* Christmas. The people at Waminda Downs didn't know her. They wouldn't murmur, *There, there, the holiday season can be tough sometimes, can't it?* She might not be through with gritting her teeth yet, but she was absolutely positively done with pity.

'I thought we'd agreed on first names, Cade.'

Very slowly, the tension eased out of him.

She turned back to stare at all the over-the-top Christmas-ness. 'My mother would find all this the height of tackiness.'

There was no denying that thought cheered her up.

'You repeat that to Ella and Holly and I'll throttle you.'

The words came out on a lazy breath but she didn't doubt their veracity. She stared down her nose at him. 'I'm the nanny, not the evil witch.'

'Just make sure you stay in character.'

She frowned and turned more fully to face him. 'You don't exactly strike me as the Santa Claus type yourself, you know?' And he didn't. Competent, calm in a crisis, perceptive, she'd peg him as all those things, but joyful and jocund? She shook her head.

'Just goes to show what you know, then.'

But he shifted on his seat and she remembered he was a father—a single father—and his first priority was making sure his daughters were looked after and happy. 'I would never ruin the magic of Christmas for any child,' she assured him.

He surveyed her again and then nodded. 'Glad that's settled.'

He still didn't strike her as Father Christmas material, but there was no questioning his devotion to his daughters. It warmed something inside her that she didn't want warmed. It made her draw back inside herself. 'When can I meet Ella and Holly?'

He eyed her thoughtfully, but eventually nodded in the direction of her car window. 'Right about now, I'd say.'

Nicola turned…and fell in love.

Four-year-old Ella and eighteen-month-old Holly wore the biggest smiles and had the most mischievous faces Nicola had ever seen, and they were dancing down the front steps of the homestead and along the path towards her in matching red and green frocks.

Good Lord! She gulped. She hadn't factored this in when she'd plotted to keep her distance and maintain her reserve as she implemented her self-improvement scheme.

She pushed out of the car, a smile spreading through her. Children, she made an amendment to her earlier plan, didn't count. Children didn't lie and cheat. Children didn't pretend to be your friend and then steal your fiancé.

She didn't need to guard her heart around children.

Cade watched Nicola greet Ella and Holly and win them over in two seconds flat.

It wasn't a difficult feat. He refused to give their perplexing nanny any credit for that. Despite all they'd been through, Ella and Holly were remarkably trusting. They'd have shown as much delight if he'd presented Jerry, the pilot, as their nanny.

But as he watched them, especially Ella, delight in Nicola's undeniably female presence, his heart started to burn. It should be their mother here. Not a nanny. And no amount of Christmas cheer could ever make that up to his children.

His hands clenched. It wasn't going to stop him from giving them the best Christmas possible, though.

He pushed out of the car in time to hear Ella ask, 'Can I call you Nikki?'

Nicola shook her head very solemnly. 'No, but you can call me Nic. All of my friends call me Nic.'

Ella clapped her hands, but at the mention of friends a shadow passed across Nicola's face. And just as he had back at the airstrip, Cade found that he wanted to chase that shadow away.

He didn't know why. His children's nanny wasn't particularly winning. She was of ordinary height and weight, perhaps veering a little more on the solid side. When she'd first emerged from the plane and had gazed around with a smile curving her lips, he'd been satisfied. When he'd shaken her hand, he'd been more than satisfied.

And then she'd become stiff and prickly and he hadn't been able to work out why yet. He was pretty sure he hadn't frightened her—given his size and the remoteness of the station he'd have understood her apprehension. He was even more certain that she hadn't wanted to turn around and go back home.

She leant her hands on her knees to talk to his daughters—ordinary hair a nondescript brown and an ordinary face. Ordinary clothes—baggy three-quarter length trousers and an oversized shirt, neither of which did anything much for her. But those eyes—there was nothing ordinary about them. Or their shadows.

Christmas wasn't the time for shadows. And Waminda Downs, this year, was not the place for them.

He hooked a thumb into the pocket of his jeans. Despite what she said, she was running from something. He was certain of it. All the background checks he'd had completed assured him that whatever it was, it wasn't criminal. The way she smiled at his daughters, her easy manner with them, told him she could be trusted with them, that his instincts hadn't let him down there.

But could she be trusted to keep her word and not create a cloud over Christmas? Ella and Holly had suffered enough. They deserved all the fun and festivity he could crowd into their days this Christmas season.

Guilt for last Christmas chafed at him, filling his mouth with bile. They hadn't had a Christmas last year. His lip curled. He should've made an effort, but he hadn't. His hands clenched. Last year he hadn't been able to pull himself out from under the cloud of Fran leaving…of her almost total abandonment of their daughters…of his failure to keep his family together. He'd let his bitterness, his anger and his despair blight last Christmas.

But not this year. This year no effort would be spared.

As he watched, Ella took one of Nicola's hands and Holly the other and they led her across to Santa's sleigh and he thought back to the expression on her face when she'd first surveyed the Christmas decorations—a kind of appalled horror.

Then, unbidden, he recalled a portion of their phone interview last month. 'Mr Hindmarsh, are you widowed, separated or divorced? I know that's a personal question and that it's none of my business, but it can have an impact on the children and I need to know about anything that may affect them.'

He'd told her the truth—that he was divorced. But...

None of the other applicants had asked that question. Nicola had been evidently reluctant to, but she'd screwed up the courage to ask it all the same. His children's best interests were more important to her than her own personal comfort. That was one of the reasons why he'd chosen her.

Nicola threw her head back now and laughed at something Ella said, and Ella laughed and Holly laughed and all three of them fell to the ground in a tangle of limbs. Nicola's face lit up as if from the inside as she gathered his children close to her and the impact slugged him in the gut, making the ground beneath his feet rock.

Blinking, he took a physical step away from the trio.

'The kids have met the new nanny then?'

He glanced down at his housekeeper, Martha Harrison—Harry for short—as she joined him. 'Yep.'

'And they seem to have hit it off.'

Nicola climbed back to her feet, looking perfectly ordinary again as she glanced towards him, her reserve well and truly back in place, and the world righted itself.

He introduced the two women. Harry nodded her approval. It should set his mind at ease. But as Nicola hugged her reserve about her all the more tightly, his unease grew.

He trailed behind as Harry led the way into the house. He waited in the kitchen as Harry and the girls showed Nicola to her quarters. 'What's eating you?' Harry asked, when she returned alone.

'Where are Ella and Holly?'

The older woman chuckled. 'Helping Nicola unpack.'

He huffed out a breath. 'Do you find her a bit…stiff?'

'She appears to be no-nonsense and low maintenance; that's good enough for me.' She shot him a glance as she put the kettle on to boil. 'Don't forget she's a long way from home and this is a lot to adjust to.'

All of those things were true, but…

Cade drew in a breath. He'd let Ella and Holly down enough these last sixteen months. His hands balled to fists. Christmas—bells and whistles…the works—that was what Waminda Downs was getting this year. And he meant to enlist Nicola's help to ensure it all went as smoothly and superbly as he'd planned.

CHAPTER TWO

AT TEN past six the next morning, dressed in running shorts and an oversized T-shirt, Nicola stepped out of the French windows of her generously proportioned bedroom and onto the veranda. She blinked in the morning sun.

Ten past six? She bit back a whimper. She'd never been a morning person.

Ten past six and it was already getting hellishly warm. It might even be too hot for a run and—

Stop that!

She lifted her chin. She would not sabotage herself before she'd even begun.

Puffing out a breath, she stretched to one side and then the other. She tried to touch her toes. She was here to change. She needed to change. She would change!

She'd exercise if it killed her. She *would* return to Melbourne better and brighter and smarter.

She gritted her teeth and stretched harder. She'd keep getting up at six a.m. if it killed her too. It gave her a good hour before she needed to make sure her young charges were up and at breakfast, and before the heat of the day settled over the place like a suffocating blanket.

At the thought of Ella and Holly, she couldn't help but smile. The two little girls were delightful. While they might've presented her with the biggest flaw in her maintain-a-dignified-distance plan, she didn't regret amending that plan to not include them.

Children didn't pretend to be your friend and then tear the heart out of your chest with treachery and double-dealing.

The bitterness of that thought took her off guard. She brushed a hand across her eyes and straightened. Diane and Brad hadn't meant to fall in love with each other. They hadn't meant to hurt her. For heaven's sake, it had all happened three months ago!

She scraped the hair off her face and pulled it back into a ponytail, concentrating on her breathing until the ache in her chest started to subside.

A lot of people who come out here are running away...

She wasn't running away. It was just…

Seeing Brad and Diane together had become harder, not easier and she didn't know why. She only knew she couldn't spend this Christmas in Melbourne while continuing to maintain her sympathetic, understanding and oh-so-mature façade. She wasn't up to indulging in the usual jolly Christmas with her friends this year. She was out of jolly.

But she'd find it again. Somehow.

She adjusted her cap as Sammy, Ella and Holly's eight-month-old Border collie pup, came skidding around the side of the house to race up to her, full of excitement and delight at the sight of her. Children *and* dogs were the flaw in her plan. He rolled onto his back and she obligingly rubbed his tummy.

'You want to come for a run, Sammy?' She straightened and set off down the back steps. He scurried after her. 'Perhaps you can give me some pointers—' she sighed '—because I don't think I have ever been for a run in my life.'

He cocked his head to one side and watched her when

she halted and planted her hands on her hips. 'Okay, Sammy, here's the plan. We'll jog to the perimeter fence—' she pointed '—and then around to that point there.' She indicated a second spot. Both spots were well away from outbuildings and cattle yards. 'Then we'll make our way back to the homestead.'

Nicola Ann, tell me you are not talking to a dog.

Nicola gritted her teeth and ignored her mother's imaginary voice.

At least you're finally going to exercise.

That almost made her turn back.

Sammy jumped up to rest his front paws against her thighs. She patted him. 'You don't care if I'm fat or frumpy, do you, Sammy?' It was one of the reasons she loved dogs...and children. Sammy wagged his tail and it gave her an absurd kind of comfort. 'Okay, then.' She hauled in a less-than-enthusiastic breath. 'Tally-ho.'

She started to jog. Her brand new sports bra was supportive, but not quite as supportive as she'd hoped. Maybe she needed to adjust the straps again. Though, if she tightened them any further she'd cut off the circulation altogether. The bra started to scratch and irritate the sides of her breasts. It hadn't done that in the fitting room. 'No pain, no gain,' she muttered to Sammy. She'd bought an identical sports bra in a size smaller for Month Two when she'd lost some weight. Both bras had been horrendously expensive. When she'd paid for them she'd told herself the expense would provide her with an added incentive to exercise. She'd thought the expense would translate into comfort too. She'd been wrong about that.

By the time she and Sammy reached the fence she was gasping for air. She sagged against a fence post. It took a concerted effort not to sink to the ground. Oh God! She glanced at her watch.

Three minutes?

No!

She shook the watch. She held it to her ear. It ticked away in perfect working order. She swallowed. 'Okay, Sammy, amended plan,' she panted. 'We jog for three minutes, then walk for three minutes.'

She set off again, fighting doubts and discouragement. She'd known this would take time. It wasn't possible to undo a lifetime of couch-potato-ness in just one day. Besides, she had a lot of chocolate sultanas to shift from her hips and thighs.

To distract herself from bursting lungs and legs that had started to burn, she forced herself to gaze at her surroundings. The quality of the light would've stolen her breath if she'd had any to spare. The clear blue of the sky and the sun low in the sky behind her outlined everything in perfect clarity. It enchanted her, even as half her attention had to remain on the path she took to avoid tussocks of grass and rocks that had definite ankle-turning potential.

She glanced at her watch and sighed. 'Time to jog again, Sammy.'

They set off at a jog, slower this time, and when her lungs started to burn again she reminded herself how much her new trainers had cost—four times what she'd paid for the bras. She *was* going to get her money's worth out of them. She could keep running for another—she glanced at her watch—one and three quarter minutes. She glanced down at her feet to admire the way the red dirt had already tarnished the brand-new perfection of her trainers when Sammy chose that moment to leap in front of her in pursuit of a grasshopper. It happened too quickly for her to avoid contact with him, to dance out of the way, to regain her balance or for anything except a full-frontal plough on her stomach through red dirt. When she came to a halt she blinked and spat out the grit that had found its way into her mouth.

Very elegant, Nicola.

True. But she took a few seconds to savour the sweet stillness of her body until Sammy, distracted from his prey by her fall, chose that moment to plaster wet licks all across her face.

'Sammy, heel!'

Sammy immediately obeyed as a shadow fell across her.

Oh, God! Cade. With a groan she rolled over and sat up. Why did her most undignified and humiliating moments have to occur in full public view?

'Are you hurt?'

'No.'

He turned and waved some signal and that was when she saw another two men—workers of Cade's, she supposed—standing outside the barn. They returned to work. The realisation that so many people had witnessed her pathetic attempt at fitness, not to mention her clumsiness, made her cheeks burn and her hands clench.

'C'mon.' Cade held a hand out to her.

Scowling at him and telling him to go away obviously wasn't an option, so she put her hand in his and let him haul her to her feet. He hitched his head in the direction of the homestead and didn't release her until she nodded her agreement.

Wiping the dirt from her face and the front of her T-shirt...and her shorts and her knees, she managed to avoid his eye. 'You don't need to escort me back.'

'Are you sure about that?'

His voice shook with laughter. She closed her eyes, more heat scorching her cheeks. She wasn't sure what was worse—him being aware of her utter mortification

or him thinking her cheeks were this red from such a pitiful amount of exercise.

'I want to make sure you haven't really hurt yourself—
twisted an ankle or a knee—but you seem to be walking
all right.'

If that was a cue to make her trip up, she had every
intention of disappointing him. 'I'm fine.' Except for a
bruised ego.

'Good. Then you and I are going to have words.'

Her heart sank. Marvellous.

He made her sit on the back steps while he inspected her
knees and elbows for scratches. 'We're a long way from a
doctor,' he said when she started to object.

She stared at the sky and tried to ignore the warmth of
his fingers on her flesh.

Finally he subsided onto the step beside her. 'So what's
with the jogging?'

Heat flared afresh in her face and neck. 'Oh, I…'

She had to look away. There was something about
those blue eyes that saw too much. He'd laugh at her. Her
lips twisted. Just like her friends in Melbourne would've
laughed if they'd seen her earlier this morning. The butt
of oh-yet-another joke.

'Nicola?'

What the hell? She lifted her chin. She was through
with turning herself inside out to please other people. 'I
thought I'd take advantage of all the wide open space and
fresh county air to…' she swallowed in readiness for his
laughter '…to try and get fit.'

She clenched her hands. Strong in body. Strong in mind.
It might not happen overnight, but she *could* work towards
it. She *could* change. She gritted her teeth. Losing her
fiancé to another woman *did not* make her a loser or a
failure.

'Dry dusty air at this time of year more like.'

She didn't say anything.

'You didn't have a water bottle with you.'

That was when it hit her—he hadn't laughed yet. And one look at his face told her he wasn't going to. He didn't think her plan of getting fit was stupid at all. Instead, he was going to tell her off for not taking a water bottle. 'I thought with it being so early and all...'

'If I see you without a water bottle the next time you go jogging, we will have serious words, you understand?'

She swallowed and nodded.

He frowned. 'It's a bit early for New Year resolutions, isn't it?'

'Getting fit and losing weight was this year's resolution,' she sighed. 'I'm trying to get it in under the wire.'

His chuckle held no malice or ridicule. It warmed her blood. 'Getting fit is an admirable goal, but losing weight...' He shook his head. 'Seems to me women get too hooked up on that stuff.'

If she'd been half a stone lighter and had taken more care with her appearance, maybe Brad wouldn't have dumped her for Diane.

Cade sent her a lazy appraisal from beneath heavy-lidded eyes and it did something ludicrous to her insides, made them light and fluttery. She didn't like it.

'Anyway, you look just fine to me,' he said with a shrug.

Her hands clenched. She didn't want to look *just fine*. She wanted to be gorgeous, stunning...confident. She wanted to knock a man's socks off.

She had a horrid sick feeling that even if she did lose half a stone and took more care with her appearance, she would never be able to achieve that anyway.

His eyes suddenly narrowed. 'I don't want you getting

obsessive about your weight while you're out here, dieting and exercising to within an inch of your life.'

She understood where Cade's concern came from. She wasn't a primary school teacher for nothing. 'I have no intention of being obsessive about anything. And I promise I will not send Ella or Holly any negative body image messages.'

He stared at her. It made her self-conscious. She made a show of looking at her watch. 'It's nearly time to get Ella and Holly up for breakfast.'

She stood and made her escape.

When Nicola and the children entered the kitchen a short time later, it was to find Cade seated at the kitchen table too. Nicola's appetite promptly fled.

He glanced up. 'You must be hungry after your morning's exertions.'

His words emerged with a lazy unconcern, but his eyes were keen and sharp. She lifted her chin. 'Absolutely.'

She might have no appetite to speak of, but there was no way she could refuse to eat breakfast. Not after their earlier conversation. The thing was, she had no intention of obsessively dieting. She just meant to avoid cakes and biscuits and chocolate sultanas and all those other yummy things while she was here.

She ate cereal and yogurt. She tried not to focus too keenly on Cade's bacon and eggs and beans on toast. Cereal and yogurt—yum, yum.

Liar.

She might not be able to summon up much enthusiasm for a high fibre, low fat breakfast, but she was well aware that Cade took note of everything that passed her lips. So she ate. It should've irked her that he watched so closely.

For some reason, though, she found it strangely comforting instead.

When they finished, he rose. 'There's something I want to show you, something I think you'll be interested in.'

Wordlessly she followed him through the house. He wore jeans that fitted him to perfection. The material stretched across lean hips and a tight butt and she couldn't drag her gaze away. Her throat hitched. Awareness—sexual awareness—inched through her. Her blood heated up and a pulse started up deep in the centre of her. She moistened her lips, curled her fingers and wondered—

No way!

She slammed to a halt. No way!

He turned back, frowned. 'What's up?'

Her racing pulse slowed as his expression filtered into her panicked brain. The denial in her throat died. She shook herself. This man didn't see her as anything other than an employee. He certainly didn't see her as an attractive, available woman. She might doubt her own strength, but she didn't doubt his.

She'd come here to toughen up, to face reality and get stronger. Lusting after her boss *was not* the answer.

'Nicola?'

She shook herself. 'I just had one of those thoughts, you know? A bolt from the blue, but... Did I leave the oven on?'

He leaned towards her. 'What? In Melbourne?'

She nodded.

'And?'

'No, I'm certain I turned it off.'

He frowned. 'You sure about that? You want to ring someone to check?'

She shook her head. 'I'm positive I turned it off.'

With a shake of his head, he continued down the corridor. He flung open a door near its far end and strode into the darkened room to lift the blinds at the window. She followed him in, glanced around and her jaw dropped. 'You have a home gym?'

There was a treadmill, an exercise bike, a rowing machine and a weight machine. Oh, this would be perfect! She walked about the room, her fingers trailing across the equipment. 'This is amazing,' she breathed. 'Is it okay if I use it?'

'Sure.' Then his face tightened up. 'Someone may as well. I don't think anyone has been in here, except to clean, since Fran left.'

Fran?

'My ex-wife and the girls' mother,' he said, answering her unspoken question.

He didn't smile. His face remained tight and it warned her not to ask questions. He obviously had his demons too. It took an effort of will not to reach out, though, and place her hand on his arm in silent sympathy. When he turned and left, she counted slowly to ten before she closed the door and followed him.

'How was your day?'

Nicola blinked and then lowered her knife and fork when she realised Cade had directed that question at her. It was nearing the end of her second full day at Waminda Downs and they were all seated around the kitchen table eating dinner. She and Cade had barely spoken since he'd shown her the home gym yesterday. 'I…um…good. Thank you,' she added belatedly. 'And…uh…you?'

He ignored that. 'Have the girls given you any trouble?'

'No!'

'So…you're settling in okay?'

'Yes, of course.' She glanced at Ella and Holly and a smile built inside her. The three of them had enjoyed a fabulous day. 'Your daughters are delightful. I can't tell you how much I enjoy their company.'

One side of his mouth hooked up. 'You don't have to. It's written all over your face.'

Was it? She sat back. Maybe that was something she should add to her list of personal-attributes-to-work-on-and-improve. She didn't want to be so easy to read. She didn't want to wear her heart on her sleeve.

She wanted to be coolly poised and self-possessed.

'It wasn't a criticism,' he said quietly.

Definitely something she needed to work on!

She tried to smooth her face out into a polite smile. 'I wanted to thank you for letting me use the home gym.'

He shrugged her gratitude aside, but his eyes started to dance. 'How's the treadmill turning out? Managing to stay on your feet?'

She nearly spluttered her mouthful of iced water across the table, but the grin he sent her made her laugh. 'That was below the belt!'

'I couldn't resist.' He took a long pull on his beer. 'Have you been having any problems with any of the equipment? There must be instruction manuals somewhere around the place.'

'It all seems to be in perfect working order. I might loathe it, but the treadmill is a cinch to operate and I don't hate it as much as that darn rowing machine.'

He stared and then he threw his head back and laughed. Harry chuckled. Ella laughed too, although Nicola suspected she had no idea what she was laughing at. She just wanted to join in. Not to be outdone, Holly let forth with a squeal

Nicola Ann, must you sound so gauche?

Inside, she cringed. She was supposed to be developing polish and self-possession, not blurting out the first thing that came into her head and sounding like an idiot, becoming the butt of the joke.

Frustration built inside her. She clenched her hands so tight her fingernails bit into her palms. Why couldn't she manage one simple thing—to think before she spoke? Was it really that hard?

Failure. Loser. Doormat.

The insults flew at her, thick and fast. Not just in her mother's voice either. Her own was the loudest.

She closed her eyes and drew in a breath. 'I'm sorry, that came out all wrong. I just meant…'

He raised an eyebrow. He'd stopped laughing but he was still grinning. That grin made her heart beat a little harder. It made it difficult for her not to grin back. She swallowed and lectured herself for the umpteenth time about dignity. 'There's absolutely nothing wrong with any of the equipment. It's just that exercise and I have an ambivalent relationship.'

'Love, you ain't the only one,' Harry said with a consoling pat to Nicola's arm. 'Now, how about I bathe the littlies while you stack the dishwasher?'

It was obvious Harry adored Ella and Holly and, if the expression on her face was anything to go by, she enjoyed bath time too. Nicola was happy to divide the chores. 'Deal.' She rose and started to clear the table.

'You promised to read me a bedtime story, Nic!' Ella reminded her. 'Don't forget.'

She planted her hands on her hips and gave an exaggerated roll of her eyes. 'How could I forget something as important as that?'

With a giggle, Ella allowed Harry to lead her away.

A glance back at the table confirmed that Cade watched her. She couldn't decipher the expression in his eyes, but it made her break out in gooseflesh and turned all her fingers to thumbs. She opened her mouth to fill the quiet, but shut it again. That kind of rattling on was neither dignified nor self-possessed. She stacked the dishwasher, and suffered his examination in silence.

'Nicola,' he said, finally breaking the silence, 'you don't strike me as the gym-junkie type.'

No, she was more a curl-up-on-the-sofa-with-a-good-book-and-a-block-of-chocolate type. Admitting that certainly wouldn't be dignified, though. 'I think we've definitely established I'm not the jogging-outside-in-the-fresh-country-air type either,' she managed with a wry, hopefully dignified smile. 'Despite what I said, I do understand the benefits of regular exercise and I am grateful for the use of your home gym.'

She poured detergent into the dishwasher and then switched it on. 'I have every intention of continuing.'

He stood. 'Come with me. There's something I want to show you.'

Last time he'd said that he'd showed her a home gym.

He grinned at her hesitation. 'You'll love it, I promise.'

Nicola smelled like strawberry jam. He'd first noticed it when he'd helped her to her feet yesterday morning. He hadn't been able to get the smell of it out of his head. He'd been craving another hit ever since. Walking beside her now towards the stables, he could drag that scent into his lungs unimpeded and drink in his fill.

Still... He glanced across at her. There was no denying that she was a hell of a puzzle. When she let her guard down her blunt honesty and self-deprecation made him laugh. She was completely unguarded around the children. She was much more reserved around him and Harry. Especially him.

And the shadows in her eyes haunted him. They reminded him of last Christmas, with all of its bleak despair and bitterness. He didn't want reminders of last Christmas. He wanted festivity and merriment and all-out Christmas cheer.

His lips twisted. He had a hunch that plugging away every day on that darn treadmill and rowing machine weren't going to improve Nicola's Christmas cheer. It might just cement those shadows in her eyes for good!

Exercise-wise, he had her pegged as a team player— basketball, cricket, softball, it probably wouldn't matter which. There wasn't a chance he'd be able to organise that out here, though. At least, not until the rest of the family arrived in a week and a half's time.

Which left him with one other option to win her over, and help dispel those shadows.

He ushered her through the door of the barn. She glanced up, spearing him with those amazing eyes. She opened her mouth, and then shut it again. He sensed the effort it took her and wondered why she didn't just ask what she so obviously wanted to.

He took her arm to guide her through the early evening dimness of the barn and through a connecting door to the stables. Her eyes widened as they walked along the line of horse stalls. Her breath quickened and beneath his fingers her skin suddenly seemed to come alive.

He dropped his hand, shook it out, and told himself to stop being stupid. Halting at a stall halfway down the row, he gestured to the horse inside. The mare whickered softly and nuzzled his hand for a treat. He fed her the lump of sugar he'd stolen from the kitchen.

'This here is Scarlett O'Hara.' He glanced down at Nicola, who was staring at the horse as if she'd never seen one before. 'She's yours to ride for the duration of your stay at Waminda Downs.'

She stared at him as if she hadn't understood. The hair at his nape started to prickle. He shoved his hands into his pockets. Did he have her pegged all wrong? It was just…

She liked kids. She liked dogs. It made sense that she'd like horses too.

He hunched his shoulders. 'I mean, if you don't want to ride that's fine. But if you do, I'm happy to teach you.'

Her eyes filled and he backed up a step. Darn it all! She wasn't going to cry, was she? He was trying to instil Christmas spirit, not histrionics.

She clasped her hands beneath her chin. 'Do you really mean that?'

Just for a moment, she reminded him of Ella. He rolled his shoulders and eyed her warily. 'Sure I do.'

She swallowed. Her eyes went back to normal. If amazing could be called normal. 'All my life,' she whispered, reaching out to rest a hand against Scarlett's neck, 'I've wanted to learn to ride.'

Her eyes suddenly shone. Her whole face came alive. She smiled. The same way she smiled at Ella and Holly. A full and open smile. A wholehearted smile. At him.

The impact hit him square in the middle of his chest. The ground beneath his feet tilted. Fire licked along his veins to pool and burn in his groin. Desire stirred inside him for the first time in sixteen months.

He took a step away from her. 'First lesson at six-fifteen sharp in the morning,' he rapped out. Then he turned on his heel and fled. He couldn't even respond to the thank you she called after him.

CHAPTER THREE

CADE had Jack, his head stockman, give Nicola her first riding lesson. He stayed away.

Curiosity, though, defeated him by mid-morning. When he saw Ella and Holly with Nicola on the lawn in the shade of one of the date palms, their tartan blanket a flash of blue and red in the sun, he took a breather from breaking in a promising young colt to make his way over to them.

As he drew nearer he could hear them singing *Waltzing Matilda*, their heads bent over…something. At least, Nicola and Ella were singing, Holly mostly la-laahed. He glanced around the garden at all the Christmas decorations and wondered why they weren't singing Christmas carols.

His gaze returned to Nicola and he chewed the inside of his lip. Without warning, Holly crawled into Nicola's lap. One of Nicola's arms went about her, cradling her easily. With her other hand she pushed the hair back from the child's forehead and dropped an easy kiss there before picking up her…crayon again. She and Ella were colouring in a gigantic picture of a billabong—complete with kangaroos, koalas, wombats, a spindly emu and…a bunyip that Ella was colouring purple and orange.

He surveyed the tableau and something warm and sweet pooled low in his belly. He'd have loved it if they sang *Jingle Bells* and coloured in a festive Santa-themed picture, but it was obvious Nicola had developed an easy relationship with his children in a very short space of time, and for that he was grateful.

'Ella,' Nicola said, halting mid-verse.

It was only when she stopped that he realised what a lovely singing voice she had.

'I have eyes in the back of my head and I do believe your daddy is standing right behind us.'

Ella spun around and with a squeal launched herself at him. He swung her up into his arms. 'Nic's magic,' she told him.

'She must be,' he agreed, wondering what had given him away.

Nicola turned then too and smiled. 'I'm a primary school teacher. Eyes in the back of one's head is a necessary prerequisite.'

Her smile didn't knock his world off its axis, didn't create a fireball of desire. He let out a long, slow breath. Last night's reaction had been nothing more than an overload of hormones—a temporary aberration. Understandable given he'd been celibate for the last eighteen months.

He did notice that her hair looked shiny in the dappled light, though, and that her skin had a healthy glow. 'How did the riding lesson go this morning?'

Her face lit up. 'Oh! It was the best fun!'

Something inside him thumped in response. He planted his legs and tried to quash it. 'I hope you didn't mind that Jack gave the lesson?'

'Not at all. He's a great teacher.'

Something in her voice, if not her face, told him she was glad he'd sent Jack in his stead. It made him want to thrust his jaw out and—

He shook himself.

'He says I'm a natural.'

It was what he'd told Cade too. When Cade had finally shown his face. It was obvious the older man liked her.

'Sore?' It was a malicious question and he didn't know where it came from.

'Not yet.'

He was going to tell her she would be in the morning, but Ella chose that moment to wriggle out of his grasp. 'Come and see our picture, Daddy. Nic brought a whole book of pictures and said we could colour in one a day if we want.'

'Any Christmas pictures?' he couldn't help asking.

The colour heightened in her cheeks, but she merely tossed her head. 'They're all native Australian bush scenes.'

'They're beautiful,' Ella announced.

He stared at Nicola and pursed his lips. 'How about a Christmas carol before I get back to work?'

'Yay!' Ella clapped her hands.

He could've sworn Nicola rolled her eyes.

Ella launched into "Rudolph the Red-Nosed Reindeer". To her credit, Nicola started on the song only a beat later. The sweetness of her voice held him spellbound.

She tossed him a crayon and broke off singing to say, 'Join in or get back to work, those are your options.'

He grinned at the school teacher bossiness of it. He started singing too and coloured a koala blue.

When they finished Ella squirmed in excitement. 'It's only twenty more sleeps till Christmas!'

Nicola didn't say anything.

Cade ruffled Ella's hair. 'That's right, pumpkin.'

'I want lots and lots of presents,' the child announced. 'I want the *Rapunzel* movie and a Barbie camper.'

Cade stifled a grin. He'd ordered the DVD and a whole load of Barbie accessories over six weeks ago. He hadn't wanted to risk the stores running out. They were stowed in the top of his wardrobe at this very moment.

'Nic!' Ella bounced some more. 'What do you want Santa to bring you?'

'I don't expect Santa to bring me anything because I'm a grown-up.'

Cade cleared his throat. 'At Waminda Downs, Santa brings everyone a present.'

Comprehension dawned in those amazing eyes.

'Every year,' Ella confided, 'he brings Harry the biggest box of chocolates and…and…something in a bottle.'

Nicola shot him a quick glance. 'Perfume?'

'Baileys Irish Cream.'

Her lips twitched. 'You know, that sounds exactly what I'd wish for too.'

'Not a Barbie camper van?' Ella said, her mouth turning down.

'I already have one. Santa brought me one when I was six.'

'Oh, okay.' Ella went back to colouring in.

Cade frowned. A box of chocolate-coated ginger and a bottle of Baileys suddenly seemed all wrong for Nicola. He shifted. 'If you could have anything, what would you ask for?'

She shook her head and shrugged. The question obviously didn't interest her and that disturbed him.

'Other than a horse,' he persisted, 'what was the one thing you asked for when you were growing up, but never got?'

She stared up at the sky, lips pursed. 'Romance novels.'

He blinked.

'I loved them when I was a teenager and when I was fourteen I asked for a collection of romance novels. What I received was a leather-bound set of the complete works of

Jane Austen. Which, technically, are romances, and don't get me wrong, I love Jane Austen, but…'

But they hadn't been what she'd asked for.

She frowned. 'I haven't read a romance novel in ages.' She glanced at him and then gave a defiant toss of her head, though he couldn't help noticing how she was careful not to jerk Holly awake. 'And no doubt my life is the poorer for it.'

Romance novels, huh?

He stared at her and his youngest daughter. 'You look like the Madonna and child.'

She snorted. 'There's nothing immaculate about me, take my word for it.'

He choked back a laugh. She stiffened and then did that stupid pulling back thing, as if she wished she hadn't said what she had, even though it was funny and had made him laugh. It ruined his mood completely.

'Time I got back to work,' he said abruptly, climbing to his feet.

'Bye, Daddy.'

He turned away, only to swing back half a second later. 'A soak in a hot bath this evening will help with the sore muscles.' And then he turned on his heel and strode off with long strides because the image that flooded his mind of Nicola stretched out in a steamy bath, her eyes heavy-lidded with pleasure, needed to be booted out again asap before the ground beneath his feet started shifting again.

He bit back a curse. Hormones might be a fact of life, but they could be darn inconvenient.

Ten days later Cade's family arrived—his mother and all her luggage on one plane, his sister and his five-year-old twin nephews on another. His brother-in-law would fly in on Christmas Eve.

This was what Cade had been dreaming of and planning for—a rowdy family Christmas full of fun and laughter and festivity.

He couldn't help noticing the way Nicola kept herself in the background, though. He'd done his best not to notice her this past week. Not that he'd been particularly successful.

He couldn't help noticing the way her gaze kept returning to the bowl of chocolate sultanas that Harry had put out as a treat, along with fruitcake and shortbread, either. She ignored the fruitcake and the shortbread, but she eyed those sultanas as if they held the answer to the universe. It made him smile. He held his breath and waited for her to seize a handful and enter into the Christmas spirit.

She didn't, even though she couldn't seem to stop her gaze from darting back to them again and again. Something in his chest started to burn.

When a bout of family Christmas carols started up, he couldn't help but notice the way her eyes dimmed, even though she kept a smile on her face. Or the way she slipped out of the French windows and onto the veranda.

Ella and Holly didn't notice. They were too entranced with their grandmother, their aunt and their cousins. Nobody else noticed either.

Cade pursed his lips and counted to ten—that was the number of days left till Christmas—and then he pushed out of his chair, had a quick word with Harry and followed Nicola into the night.

Nicola stared out at the darkness and couldn't believe how many stars this Outback night sky held. She had never seen so many stars. Around on this side of the veranda, away from the light spilling from doors and windows and where she could barely hear the Christmas carols, the stars gleamed bigger and brighter.

Away from all that Christmas merriment, the burn surrounding her heart started to ease too.

And then her sixth sense kicked in—Cade—and a different kind of burning started up in her veins. A heat she didn't want. A heat she certainly didn't trust.

She didn't turn from the railing. 'You should be in there with your family and enjoying this time with them.'

'So should you.'

She turned at that. 'They're not my family, Cade. Besides, I think it's nice for Ella and Holly to have a chance to focus on their grandmother, aunt and cousins without me getting in the way. And don't worry, I'm wearing my watch. I'll put them to bed in another half an hour.'

'Three things.' His voice cut the air. 'One, you're not in the way. Two, for as long as you're at Waminda you're part of the family. Three, I asked Harry to put the girls to bed. I saw how much you helped her with dinner.'

His high-handedness irked her. She didn't like his tone much either. Last month the old Nicola would've shrugged it off and tried to ignore it, but not the new improved version of Nicola McGillroy. No, sirree.

'One—' she held up a finger '—I'm here to do a job and I don't need anyone else to do it for me. I can carry my own weight.' She just wasn't prepared to carry anyone else's any more. 'And two, I should be allowed a few moments' quiet time every now and again without you jumping on me with that you're-ruining-Christmas tone in your voice.'

She had no intention of ruining Christmas for Cade and his family. It was why she'd stolen from the living room earlier. All that Christmas gaiety had filled her with such unexpected longing it had stolen her breath and knocked her sideways… For a moment she'd thought she might burst into tears.

She shuddered. How would she have explained that?

'I didn't mean to jump on you.'

The shock in his voice shamed her. All he was trying to do was give his kids and family a nice Christmas. Her hang-ups weren't his fault. She gripped her hands together. She only had to put up with all this Christmas cheer for another week and a half.

Fortitude was never your strong point was it, Nicola Ann?

She gritted her teeth. This wasn't much different from keeping a class entertained at school. She could do that with one hand tied behind her back. This was just a job.

She dragged in a breath. 'Okay then, let's get back to it.' She clapped her hands. 'I've taken the three deep breaths I needed to resist that bowl of chocolate sultanas. My healthy eating plan is still intact. Besides, I don't think we've had a rendition of "Good King Wenceslas" yet and that's one of my favourites.'

'No.'

The single word brought her up short, as did the hand curling about her upper arm and preventing her from going anywhere. 'No?' Why not? She'd just agreed to what he wanted, hadn't she?

'This isn't just a job!'

She begged to differ, but wisely kept her mouth shut. Cade's vehemence ensured that. Parents hated reminders that teaching little Johnny or Jane was actually a job and not the blessing and privilege they considered it.

Besides, if she pointed out to Cade that her title was in fact Nanny and not Friend or Family Member, it would give him the wrong impression. It would make it sound as if she didn't really care for Ella and Holly when she did. She adored them.

It didn't change the fact that this was still a job, though, and that no matter how much Cade and his family welcomed her into their fold, it still didn't make her one of them.

It wasn't anything to be bitter about. It wasn't anything to be hurt about. It was the truth, plain and simple.

Oh, but how she wished she had a family like his!

The warmth of his hand on her arm filtered into her consciousness. The pulse in her throat fluttered to life. 'Unhand me, sir.' Although she struggled for light, the words came out husky.

Cade released her, but he stood so close she could smell the clean scent of soap on his skin. She gulped. Starlit night, a guy and girl alone…

Stop it! She knew her musings were nonsensical and that in all likelihood Cade hadn't even noticed the stars, or the fact that she was a woman. It still took a concerted effort to ease back a step when, by rights, the thought should've had her running for the hills.

Classic rebound reaction, she told herself, her lips twisting in mockery at her own weakness. 'If you don't want me to return inside, what is it you would like me to do?'

'I want you to listen.'

He didn't say anything else. A long moment passed. 'To?' she prompted.

He took her arm again and all that warm maleness flooded her senses. The latent strength of him set her nerves jangling. He led her to a bench, urged her to sit and then released her again.

'I want to tell you why Christmas is so important for me, for Waminda Downs, and for Ella and Holly this year.'

Instinct told her that she didn't want to hear what he

was about to say. She wanted to get up and walk away. She had enough issues of her own to deal with, without adding his to the score. But when she looked up into his face, she found she didn't have the strength to do that. Just for a moment he looked as tired and defeated as she felt each morning when she woke up. Before she'd had a chance to remind herself that she was on a cattle station in the Outback and that she had a riding lesson that very morning to look forward to.

He eased down beside her. She studied him for a moment—the downturned mouth, the slumped shoulders, the way it seemed an effort to draw breath into his lungs, and a lump formed in her throat. It was obvious he needed to share this with someone. Why not the temporary nanny who'd be gone again in six weeks' time?

It's just a job, she reminded herself.

But it felt like so much more and she didn't know when that had happened. She bit back a sigh. So much for keeping her distance.

He was sitting beside her on the bench in the warm night air, their arms and shoulders not quite touching. This time she didn't prompt him. She sat there and stared out at the sky, breathing him in and waiting.

Finally he spoke. 'Last Christmas was our first Christmas without Fran.'

Her heart clenched at the pain in his voice.

'She'd left about four months earlier, but…'

He dipped his head and raked his fingers through his hair. She reached out and laid a hand on his forearm. The muscles tensed beneath her fingertips. 'You really don't have to tell me any of this, you know?'

He laid his other hand over hers and squeezed it, and then he placed her hand back in her lap. It felt like a rejection but she didn't know why. She stared straight out in front of her and focused on her breathing.

'I think it's probably best if you know.'

She didn't say anything, just gave a curt nod.

'Fran left us all here at Waminda in late August and went to Brisbane.' He paused. 'I thought she just needed a break. It can be hard getting used to the isolation of a cattle station, and with two small children—one barely three months old—I could understand her going a bit stir-crazy.'

Nicola frowned. 'You mean…you're saying she left Ella and Holly here?'

Even in the dimness she could see him smile, but it didn't hold any mirth. 'That's what I'm saying.'

She bit her tongue and turned back to stare straight out in front of her. She couldn't imagine anyone wanting to leave Ella and Holly behind, not for any reason. Unless… 'Post-natal depression?'

'That's what she told me. She was seeing a therapist. I even spoke to the damn therapist.'

She understood his frustration, his anger, but… 'She wouldn't have been able to help it, you know.'

The smile he sent her held a world of weariness. 'Depression was something I was fully prepared to deal with, Nicola. I'd have done anything I could've to help her through it. I set her up in an inner city apartment so she could see her therapist as often as she needed, and so she could have the change of scenery she claimed to so badly need. I wired her as much money as she asked for. I took the girls to visit as often as I could, and all the while I made endless excuses for her distance and her erratic behaviour. I mean depression, right? It's out of her control. I might be doing it tough, but she was doing it a whole lot tougher, right?'

With each *right* his voice rose. She swallowed and nodded. 'Right,' but her voice came out on a breath of uncertainty. She gripped the edge of the bench and turned to face him fully. 'But?'

He rested his head back against the wall behind him and closed his eyes. 'But it was all a lie.'

'A lie?'

'A blind, a decoy, a red herring to throw me off the trail of what was really happening.'

Her mouth had gone as dry as the soft red sand of the Outback. 'What was really happening?'

'For three months she let me go on thinking that our marriage had a chance, but all the while she was planning to leave me and Ella and Holly for another man.'

She couldn't stop her jaw from dropping. 'She strung you along for three months?'

His eyes opened. His lips twisted and he pointed to his forehead. 'Can't you see the word Stupid branded here?'

'You weren't stupid! You trusted her, supported her and… You were married, for heaven's sake!' She pressed fingertips to her temples. Thank God Brad had dumped her before they'd married.

'Apparently returning to Waminda was her backup plan if things didn't work out with her Texan millionaire.'

She eyed him for a moment, swallowed. 'I guess they did. Work out, that is.'

'They did.'

'I guess telling you you're better off without her isn't any comfort at all?'

'A little.' This time his smile was genuine. It faded. 'But Ella and Holly aren't better off without a mother.'

She shook her head. 'No.' She couldn't keep the horror out of her voice. 'Whose decision was that?' She understood Cade's anger, his bitterness, but would he prevent his ex-wife from seeing their children?

'Hers,' he replied in a dead voice and she immediately kicked herself for what she'd just thought. She'd seen him with his children. He didn't have that kind of spite in him.

'Quote: "I'm not taking any extra baggage like children from a previous marriage into my new life. Chip wouldn't like it."'

'God!' She didn't try to hide her disgust. 'Where on earth did she pick him up from?'

'The Internet.'

She slouched back. 'Poor Ella and Holly.'

'You said it.'

And poor Cade.

She glanced at him, and roused herself. 'The girls,' she ventured, 'seem to have bounced back okay. Ella is remarkably well adjusted considering all she's been through.' The young girl could be clingy at times, but she understood why now. Holly was still just a baby. Who knew how this would affect her in the years to come?

'I feel we've finally come out the other side.'

His voice told her it had been hell.

'And this Christmas is a…a signal of a new start?'

'It's an attempt to make up to them in some small way for the wretchedness of the last year.' His hands clenched. 'It's my attempt to make amends for all but ignoring Christmas last year.'

If Fran had left him in late August and then strung him along for three months… 'Fran broke up with you in late November?'

'Early December,' he said shortly.

'Oh, Cade, you can't blame yourself for last Christmas. It takes time to adjust to a shock like that.'

'That's no excuse for not giving Ella and Holly one day of brightness amid all that upheaval. My mother and sister tried to talk me into spending the holidays with them in

Brisbane. But Brisbane was the last place I wanted to be, especially knowing that Fran was so close and yet didn't want to see her own daughters.'

He shook his head. He didn't say anything more…not that he needed to.

'I'm sorry for all you've been through. If it helps any, you're giving not only Ella and Holly the kind of Christmas dreams are made of, but your mother, sister and nephews as well.'

He sent her a sidelong glance. 'And yet the one thing I can't seem to give them is a nanny brimming over with the joy of the season.'

The criticism stung. She thought she'd been doing fine and dandy on the Christmas front.

'Considering the way I behaved last year, I realise I'm the last person who should be criticizing someone else's Christmas spirit.'

But it wasn't going to stop him from finding fault with her, right? 'So you're a pot and I'm the kettle?'

He turned to her. 'Why are you spending Christmas at Waminda Downs instead of in the bosom of your family or with your friends—with the people you love?'

It was the sheer gentleness of his voice that was her undoing, an inherent understanding that she was dealing with a hell of her own.

She opened her mouth and he leant forward to press a finger to her lips. 'No nonsense about wanting to experience the majesty of the Outback or searching for adventure or anything else I could get from a travel brochure. At least give me that much respect.'

To her horror, tears filled her eyes. This man had just shared the breakdown of his marriage with her so she could understand why Christmas meant so much to him this year.

The least she could do was explain why Christmas was low on her personal landscape.

She swallowed and nodded. He removed his hand and leant back again.

She didn't speak until she was sure she had her voice back under control. 'I'm not spending this Christmas in the bosom of my family because there's only my mother and my aunt, and my mother's bosom isn't very…um…warm.'

'I'm sorry.'

She shrugged. 'We come from money but the one thing my mother couldn't buy was the daughter she'd always wanted.' She blew out a breath and tried to smile. 'I'm afraid I've been a sore disappointment to her. I was never the blonde, svelte ballerina type she'd have liked to see blossom into a society princess who loved fashion and charity lunches.' Her lips twisted. 'Oh, and the shock and horror of it all when I decided to earn my own living. Why on earth did I have to choose something as unglamorous as teaching? Couldn't I at least have had the consideration to study Law or Medicine? At least she'd have been able to brag about those.'

He rested his elbows on his knees. 'Is she blind?' he demanded.

'No, she just sees the world through her own eyes and can't comprehend anyone else's view of it.' She laughed. 'Nicola Ann, you're twenty-seven and too old to be gallivanting around the countryside as a nanny looking after someone else's children. Think of all that dust and heat… and the flies! What on earth will I tell my friends?'

'She said that?'

'Verbatim.' She glanced down at her hands. 'Christmas lunch with my mother and aunt is an ordeal. They spend at least an hour picking over my myriad flaws and the perceived mistakes I've made for the year. Given my start in life and all... Yadda yadda yadda. You get the picture.'

'I do.' His voice was grim.

'And this year I just couldn't face it. Normally I only survive that lunch with my mother because of the promise of a rollicking good party with my friends in the evening—my Christmas highlight.'

'And that's not happening this year?'

Oh, it was happening all right. She just wouldn't be a part of it.

'Nicola?'

She hadn't meant to reveal her troubles to anyone while she was here at Waminda Downs. She'd promised herself that she was through with being an object of pity. And she was. 'I don't want this going any further. I don't want you telling your family or Harry or Jack or anyone about this.'

'That always went without saying. But you have my word of honour.'

Even now she knew she could pull back—plead a headache and retire to her room. Flee to her room. But she suddenly found she didn't want to. She wanted to lance some of the poison that blackened her thoughts until she could taste the bitterness in her mouth. She wanted to hurl it into the darkness where the night could swallow it and hopefully destroy it.

She pulled in a breath that made her whole frame shake. 'Right now I should be in the middle of wedding preparations. *My* wedding preparations.'

His head snapped back. 'You're engaged?'

'Was. Past tense.'

'Hell, I'm sorry. I...'

He trailed off like so many of her friends had when they'd heard the news.

'He dumped me for another woman and, yes, before you

say it, I agree it's better to have found that out now than after we were married.'

'It's still a tough blow and a lot to deal with, but...'

She glanced up. 'Yes?'

'I'd have thought being with your friends at a time like this would've been the best thing. You could've blown your mother off with some excuse or other.' He rolled his eyes. 'I mean, I can just imagine her comments on a broken engagement, but having the support and understanding of your friends would've been invaluable, wouldn't it?'

She laughed and the bitterness of it cut deep into her. 'I'm sorry I left out one tiny detail. My fiancé dumped me for my best friend.'

CHAPTER FOUR

NICOLA couldn't look at Cade after she'd uttered those words. His shocked intake of breath told her all she needed to know.

Along with the silence.

She hated that kind of silence. She'd dealt with too much of it these past three months. 'We're all still friends. Brad and Diane didn't mean for it to happen. They didn't mean to hurt me.'

'How very adult of you,' he ground out wryly.

She grimaced. He was right. She sounded like a B-grade actor in some corny nineteen-eighties telemovie.

When she glanced at him she recognised the flare of anger in his eyes and she knew it was directed at Brad and Diane, not at her. And God forgive her, but it made her feel good.

The thing was, they hadn't meant to hurt her. She knew that.

But they had.

They'd crushed something vital inside her and she didn't know how to get it back.

'They announced their engagement last month and that's when I realised I couldn't spend Christmas in Melbourne this year. Without meaning to, I'd ruin it for everyone. A lot of our set are angry with them, but are following my lead because I've asked them to. If I'd stayed I wouldn't have been able to keep the brave face up. It would've created a division in the group and I don't want that. It's not fair to force people to take sides.'

'So you applied for a job and came out here.'

Her lips twisted and an apology welled inside her. 'With all my Christmas spirit, I'm afraid.' And that had hardly been fair either, had it? She glanced down at her hands. 'When I arrived you asked me if I was running away from something. I'm not running away. I'm just taking a break and gathering my resources before I have to face it all again.'

He nodded, but didn't say anything.

She bit back a sigh. 'I'm sorry. I can see now that was hardly fair of me. I thought I'd be in the background out here and not of much consequence.' Her actions suddenly seemed horribly selfish and self absorbed.

Cade still didn't say anything.

She winced. 'Do you want me to leave?'

He didn't answer that either. Her heart started to pound. She glanced at him. He glared back at her. 'So what the hell is with the getting fit and losing weight thing?'

Oh.

She swallowed and stared out into the night, unable to look at him. The glory of the stars still awed her. She wanted to reach out and touch one, clasp it in her hand and make a wish.

A childish fantasy, but no more childish than believing she could've built a life with Brad.

'Nicola?'

She bit back a sigh. 'I've come up with a plan to make myself over and improve myself.'

He shifted on his seat. 'You've what?'

She was proud she didn't flinch at his incredulity. She

kept her eyes fixed on the brightest star. 'Strong in body, strong in mind. At least, that's the idea.'

'What are you hoping to achieve?'

He spoke those words much quieter and it took an effort to keep her focus on the starlit sky and not turn to him. 'I want to look better, I want to feel better, and I want people to stop looking at me like I'm a victim. I want to develop some smarts. I didn't see the Brad and Diane thing coming at all. It was a bolt from the blue.' She straightened. 'And I want to develop some…some poise and self-possession. That way everybody will stop feeling sorry for me, they'll respect me, and I'll be able to…move on.'

'Nicola?'

She gave in and looked at him.

'Change is fine, but don't take it too far. Making sure you're not taken for granted doesn't have to translate into being unfriendly.'

Her jaw dropped. 'Is that how I've come across?'

One of those broad shoulders of his lifted. She went back over all their earlier encounters. She considered the way she'd kept everyone here at arm's length and her cheeks started to burn. 'I'm not getting the balance right, am I?'

'It could use some work.'

Changing was proving a whole lot harder than she'd initially envisaged. 'What I need is a fairy godmother to wave a magic wand or a genie to grant me three wishes,' she sighed.

'And what would you wish for?'

'To be fit and healthy.' Which translated to thin, but that seemed far too shallow to say out loud. 'To have the poise and chutzpah to carry myself with confidence,' regardless of how she was actually feeling. 'And…and to stop burying my head in the sand, to realise what's right under my nose and face reality.' And to stop feeling so angry, she added silently.

'That's all very noble,' he drawled. 'Now give me the other wish list.'

She spun to face him. How could he know? And then she remembered all he'd been through with Fran and his marriage breakup. Her mouth dried. 'The less admirable list?'

'That's the one.'

How badly would he think of her if she uttered those things out loud? Then she remembered she was through with caring what people thought of her.

She frowned. She was through with caring *so much* about what people thought of her. She would find the right balance. Eventually.

'Okay, out with it.'

She swallowed. 'I really, really, *really* want to look good at their wedding. I want them to feel bad that their happiness has come at my expense, but at the same time I want them to admire me and…and to miss me. Because, yes, while we're still friends, things have changed and no matter how hard I try I can't make them go back to the way they were before.'

He stared at her. She pushed her hair off her face and tried to shove her self-consciousness to a place where it couldn't plague her. But… He thought her shallow now, didn't he? And weak. She tossed her head. 'What?' she demanded, losing the battle.

'You didn't ask for Brad back.'

'I don't want him back.' If she said it often enough, eventually she'd believe it. And it was partly true. Who wanted a cheating spouse who didn't really love them? But…

Oh, how she ached for the promise of the life they

could've had—the home, the babies, the laughter. The belonging.

Her eyes burned. She blinked hard and forced her chin up. 'I want a hot date for the wedding. That way, no one will feel sorry for me.' Not that she had any idea where to find a hot date, mind.

'You want to look gorgeous. You want to be able to hold your head high, and you want a hunky man at your side.'

She nodded.

'None of those things are ignoble.'

She glanced at him and swallowed. 'I was going to say that the moment Diane saw me again I wanted her to worry that I could steal Brad away from her if I chose to, and that the moment Brad clapped eyes on me again he'd start to wonder if he'd chosen the wrong woman.'

'But?'

'But it's not true. Not really. I just get irrationally angry sometimes.' She glanced down at her hands. 'I do actually hope their marriage is happy and strong. I wish them both well.'

He sat back and stared. 'The anger isn't irrational.'

A part of her agreed, but… 'It comes out of the blue sometimes when I'm not expecting it. It's so…bitter and unforgiving. I hate feeling like that.'

'It'll get easier with time.'

She hoped so.

He was silent for a while, then leant forward to rest his elbows on his knees. 'How about you and I make a deal?'

She raised her eyebrows. 'A deal?'

'I will help you get fit, and I'll do what I can to aid your makeover plans…and I'll also be your date for the wedding.'

Her jaw dropped. He'd be her date? But… An immediate image of her friends' surprise—Diane and Brad's surprise—flooded her.

'And in return…'

She pressed a hand to her chest to counter its sudden and erratic pounding. 'In return?' Her voice had gone hoarse.

'And in return you'll help me make this Christmas and the holidays fabulous for Ella and Holly, and the rest of my family.'

Her heart kept right on pounding. 'Asking you to be my date, Cade, is too much.'

'Do you have someone else in mind for the job?'

'Well, no, but—'

'Call it a Christmas bonus.'

She wanted him as her date for that far-off wedding. His mere presence would fill her with confidence. Somewhere in the past week or so, his confidence and self-possession had become her blueprint for what she was working towards.

She cocked her head. 'Okay, be specific. Exactly how is my Christmas cheer supposed to manifest itself?' She was getting a lot out of this deal. She needed to know she could deliver her side of the bargain.

'Help me and the kids decorate the house. Sing Christmas carols. Help the kids write letters to Santa. Help Ella make gifts for the family. And…and take part in all the revelry, whatever form that takes—charades, telling Christmas stories, whatever. I want you to act like one of the family.'

He would help with her makeover plan, plus he would be her date to the dreaded wedding, and all she had to do was be Christmassy? She imagined the expressions on Brad and Diane's faces when she turned up at the wedding with Cade. She knew Diane so well. She knew exactly what Diane would think—*hot, gorgeous hunk*. Oh, yes, that would be *very* satisfying.

Shallow, yes, but satisfying as well.

To no longer be the object of all those furtive glances, those consoling pats on the arm, those 'poor Nicola' comments! Something inside her lifted.

Was he serious—all she had to do was be Christmassy? She stuck out a hand before he could change his mind. 'You have yourself a deal.'

He closed his hand around hers. His grip was firm and she could feel the way he tempered his strength so as to not crush her fingers. He didn't let go again immediately and her heart started up its silly pounding and erratic fluttering again.

'Nicola...'

Her name was a caress in the warm night air. Brad had never uttered her name like that. Her heart pounded louder, harder. 'Yes?'

'I know your confidence has taken a beating, and I respect the fact that you'd like to get fit, but as for your weight...and everything else, I don't think you need to change a damn thing.'

For a moment she actually believed he was sincere.

Oh, Nicola Ann, the man's a comedian!

She flinched as she imagined her mother's scornful laughter. She pulled her hand from his and leapt up, moving across to the nearest veranda post. She wrapped her hands around it. 'Is that a way of saying you'll help me with my makeover plan, but as you don't think I need to change there's nothing you need to actually do?'

'Damn it, no!'

He shot to his feet and strode across to her, gripping her chin in his hand to force her to meet his gaze. 'You're a hell of an infuriating woman, you know that?'

Infuriating was better than pitiful.

His face softened as he stared down at her. 'Sorry,' he murmured, his touch on her chin becoming gentle. 'I shouldn't have snapped.'

'I…um…' She swallowed. 'I'm probably a touch sensitive,' she allowed.

'A person doesn't bounce back just like that after the kind of blow you've suffered, Nicola. But you don't need to change and eventually you'll see I'm right.'

She doubted that, but she couldn't utter a single sound. Under his fingers her skin had leapt to life. His thumb traced the skin beneath her bottom lip. It made her drag in a breath that made her whole body tremble.

'You have the most amazing eyes I have ever seen,' he murmured.

It wasn't her eyes he was staring at, but her mouth. And he was staring at it as if he was hungry, as if he was starved. That gaze held her spellbound. It promptly cut off her mother's disbelieving comments and hurtful contradictions. She should step away. She should flee. She knew that in some deep, dark recess of her mind, but her hand curled about the veranda post all the more tightly to anchor her into place.

Cade had become the brightest star in the night and she wanted to bask in the glow of his warmth and his…desire. Even if for only ten seconds more.

His free hand travelled down the post until he found her hand. He closed it around hers. He stepped in so close their chests touched. 'You smell like strawberry jam.'

She tried to ask him if that was a good thing, but her throat wouldn't work. All that happened was her lips parted.

And that he saw them part.

And knew what it meant.

His eyes glittered. His mouth took on a wolfish edge of satisfaction. He brushed his thumb over her bottom lip. She gasped and a low rumble of approval emerged from his chest.

'Amazing eyes,' he repeated. 'Hair that shines in the starlight.' His thumb stopped alternately tormenting and pleasing her lips as his hand drifted around the back of her neck to slide into the hair at the base of her skull. He tipped her head back so he could devour her face with his gaze, and she let him.

He was going to kiss her. She knew he was going to kiss her. She hovered between breaths, waiting for it, waiting to welcome it...hungering for it.

And from the glittering satisfaction in his eyes she could tell that he'd read that thought in her eyes—that she wanted it as much as he did, that there would be no argument or resistance.

His mouth descended. The pressure of his hand at her nape partly lifted her to meet him, demanded that she meet him.

And she did, with her lips ready to taste him completely.

The kiss was not tentative on either side—it was assured and demanding. Nicola was twenty-seven years old but she had never had such a blatantly adult kiss in all that time.

Had never enjoyed such a blatantly adult kiss. There was no game playing and no teasing or preliminaries. A question had been asked. An answer given. And then the thorough enjoyment, a wholehearted participation in the slaking of a mutual need.

And the pleasure rocked her to her toes. She clutched his upper arms, not aware of when she'd moved, his heat and strength rippling through the thin cotton of his shirt to her palms and fingers, filling her with a sense of invincibility. His arm snaked around her waist—to pull her more firmly against him or to give her support? She didn't know and she didn't care. She was simply grateful that it gave her the freedom to dance her fingers across his throat, to smooth them over his shoulders and then plunge them into his hair to pull him closer.

The kiss went on and on and it filled her with energy and strength and the yearning for more…so much more!

Eventually Cade lifted his head, but he didn't remove his arm from around her waist. She didn't remove hers from around his neck. She met his gaze head on. With Cade she didn't need to be coy.

His eyes didn't waver from hers. 'If this goes on for much longer we're going to get to the point of no return,' he rasped out.

She nodded.

His chest, pressed to hers, rose and fell. 'I need to think about that.'

So did she.

In unspoken agreement they unclasped each other. Nicola moved back to the bench as reaction set in and her knees started to shake.

Did she want to take this any further? Did she want to go all the way with Cade? Oh, her body was in no doubt but what about her brain…and her heart?

He didn't turn from where she'd left him. 'I'm not ready for anything serious.' He spoke to the night, but she knew the words were meant for her.

After all he'd revealed about his marriage and Fran, she wasn't surprised. 'I'm not either.' It was the truth.

He turned. She could read the question in his eyes.

She'd come out here to focus on getting her life back together. A holiday fling, however brief, would deflect her from that. And her plan for self-improvement was important to her. She didn't want to be the doormat her friends thought her or the failure her mother considered her.

She stood, her knees finally steady. 'No.'

She sensed the relief that flashed through him, along with the frustration. He nodded once. He didn't say anything.

'If I slept with you it'd be partly as revenge on Brad and Diane. You might say you wouldn't care about that.' Men were all hormones and any excuse, right? 'But I'd care.'

'No, Nicola, you're wrong. I'd resent being used like that.'

'The other thing is, I don't want to go falling for you on the rebound. My emotions are all over the place at the moment and I don't trust them. I'm not ready for anything serious and I can say that till I'm blue in the face, but...'

'But sometimes it's impossible to keep things emotion-free and uncomplicated.'

'Neither one of us needs complicated right now.' The blood burned in rebellion in her veins. She swallowed and told herself she was doing the right thing. 'Besides,' she croaked, 'you have the girls to consider.'

'I do.'

'And I don't much trust the whole notion of romantic love any more. I think it's a bubble that eventually gets burst. Down the track, hopefully, I'll meet someone and get married because I want children, but I mean to go into the marriage with wide eyes and a clear head. My head at the moment isn't clear.'

They eyed each other warily. 'I'm sorry,' she offered, because it felt as if she should apologise.

He gave an emphatic shake of his head. 'The first lesson in PD101 is to never apologise for something that isn't your fault. This isn't anyone's fault. Never apologise for being honest.'

'PD?'

'Personal Development.'

That sounded much grander than a makeover plan. 'Personal development,' she murmured. 'I like it.' With that she started to edge away. She might have finally screwed her head on right, but it didn't counter the effect of Cade's continued proximity. Her body clamoured for the feel of him, the touch of his lips and hands—his hardness pressed tight against her softness. And rather than diminishing, it was starting to increase. 'I'll…um…say goodnight then.'

'Nicola?'

She turned at the question, adrift between him and the French windows to her bedroom. She clasped her hands together tightly.

'When you said you wanted to go into marriage with a clear head, what did you mean?'

She didn't move back towards him. That would be foolish. With the moon behind him, and from this distance, she couldn't see his face clearly. 'From what I've seen of relationships, there are those who do the giving and those who do the taking. Until now I've been one of the givers. In the future I'm going to be a taker. I mean to get precisely what I want out of any marriage.'

'Take the poor sod to the cleaners, so to speak?' The air whistled between his teeth. 'Thank God you called a halt to things just then. They could've gotten darn messy.'

And just like that he'd made her laugh. 'Don't worry, Cade. You would never have made it into my sights.' He was a lot of things, but a poor sod wasn't one of them. 'Given all you've been through, I doubt you'd ever want to dip your toe in matrimonial waters again.'

'Damn right.'

'So I wouldn't have made the elementary mistake of thinking you were available.'

He shifted. She still couldn't see his face clearly. 'It seems to me that if your main reason for marrying is to have children, you could dispense with the middleman and use IVF instead. No point in putting yourself in a miserable relationship with a man you would neither respect or trust.'

She stilled. 'You know, you've got a point there.' She could dispense with the mess of romance for good. It was an intriguing idea. 'Goodnight, Cade.' She turned and headed for her room. This time he didn't call her back.

Cade didn't waste any time, he got to work on his side of the bargain the very next day. Nicola's opinion of the human race was at an understandable low and he didn't want to add to it. He wanted to prove to her that some people did keep their promises.

While she was busy outside with all four children playing some game that involved a lot of running, a lot of freezing and a whole lot of laughing, he dragged his mother and Delia into the kitchen, where Harry was preparing lunch.

Verity Hindmarsh glanced out of the window, attracted by the laughter of the children, and smiled. 'Nicola is a gem.'

'That she is,' Harry huffed.

'Awfully quiet, though,' Delia mused. 'But wonderful with Jamie and Simon.'

Jamie and Simon had recently turned five and had the kind of energy that could make Cade dizzy just watching them. Dee was enjoying the advantage of having another person to help out with them. Not that Cade blamed her or begrudged her, but he meant to make sure Nicola didn't get lumped with more than her fair share of the work.

'Nicola is what I want to talk to you about.' As one they turned to survey him. He did his best not to fidget. 'I found out recently that it's not just the Outback she's never experienced, but a big family Christmas. It's just her and her mother who is rather over-critical, from what I can make out.'

Harry stopped chopping salad vegetables to glance out of the window. 'Well, now, that makes sense. Probably why she's got such a bee in her bonnet about exercising and losing weight.'

At the words 'losing weight', Harry instantly had the other two women's attention.

'She tried jogging around the property in the early morning, but…' she flicked a glance at Cade '…but that didn't work out so well. So Cade set her up in Fran's old home gym.'

He didn't know why, when all three women turned to look at him, he wanted to roll his shoulders and back out of the room. 'Someone may as well use it,' he mumbled. 'She's no gym junkie, though.'

Harry sliced through a lettuce with evident satisfaction. 'So when he found out she'd always wanted to learn to ride, he set her up with Jack for lessons each morning.'

'That was a lovely thing to do,' his mother said. While he was no longer a seven-year-old, he found himself momentarily basking in the warmth of her approval. The kind of approval it seemed that Nicola had never received. 'But why aren't you teaching her yourself?'

That wasn't something he was prepared to get into. 'She and Jack have hit it off. He's enjoying it.'

'And Jack's not getting any younger,' Harry observed.

'He's still more than capable of putting in a full day's work.'

'Darling—' his mother laid a hand on his arm, her eyes warm with a mixture of relief and delight '—I thought we'd lost you for ever after everything Fran did, but I can see now that's not the case. I can't tell you how happy I am to see you being your old self again.'

Fran's betrayal had left a mark that would never go away. It had killed something inside him. But for Ella and Holly's sake, he'd had to pull himself together. It occurred to him now just how much he'd put these three women through in the last year or so, but they'd stood beside him through it all. He glanced out of the window. He was lucky.

'I know it's been a bit of a long haul.' He grimaced. 'I'm sorry if I—'

'No apologies necessary,' his mother cut in. 'Just tell me you're over the worst of it.'

He nodded. 'I'm through with looking back and trying to work out where it went wrong. I'm not sure I'll ever understand why Fran did what she did, but it's time to look towards the future. From here on it's onwards and upwards.'

'And does a particular pretty nanny have anything to do with that?' Delia asked archly.

'For God's sake, Dee, not everything is about sex and romance,' he muttered in disgust.

Dee didn't look convinced.

'She's a bit of a lost soul is all and I thought we might be able to...'

She cocked a wicked eyebrow again. 'To?'

He refused to rise to the bait. 'To make her feel at home here. To take her under our wing and...and make her feel better about herself.'

'I think that's a lovely plan,' his mother said.

Cade shrugged and then glared at his sister. 'One thing's for sure, Nicola certainly doesn't think she's pretty, and she thinks she's fat.'

Verity sighed. 'Don't we all.'

Harry snorted. 'And some of us are a bit on the heavy side, but I know my worth.'

Dee had gone to the window. 'She is pretty, but in a quieter way than Fran's flashiness.'

He didn't like the way she spoke about Nicola and Fran in the same sentence. It seemed wrong somehow. He didn't say anything, though. He could just imagine what Dee would make of it if he did.

'A haircut,' she said, suddenly swinging back to face them. 'Something that would make the most of her eyes. Mum?'

Verity hadn't trained as a hairdresser, but she had a knack for it. When she'd lived at Waminda Downs all the station women in a three hundred kilometre radius would come to get their hair done by her.

Dee touched her hair. 'I brought along a couple of bottles of permanent colour and a highlighting kit. I was hoping you'd do my hair for me while we were here, but we can use it on Nicola instead.'

He glanced from one to the other. They wanted to change her hair colour? There was nothing wrong with her hair.

Verity joined Dee at the window. 'I believe I know the exact style that would suit her.'

'Those clothes,' Dee sighed.

'Far too baggy,' her mother agreed.

Harry winked at him. 'Sounds like our Nic's in good hands.'

She wasn't his anything. He wanted that crystal-clear, but…

'I don't want you bullying her into something she doesn't want.'

His mother swung around. 'Of course not, darling. Harry, can you look after the children for a couple of hours this afternoon? Dee and I will help with dinner in return.'

'No probs at all.'

'And I don't want you wrecking her.' He thrust his jaw out. 'She's not a Barbie doll. Don't go making her look all plastic and…and fake.'

Like Fran. The words hung in the air.

The three women exchanged glances but didn't say anything.

'And…and don't make her feel like a charity case either.' She'd hate that and he didn't want to do anything that would make her feel uncomfortable. He hadn't broken her confidence about her two-timing fiancé and backstabbing girlfriend, but he had verbalised his opinion of her mother and he was pretty sure she wouldn't have appreciated that. He shifted his weight from his heels to the balls of his feet. Now that he had his mother and Dee on board, conversely he wanted to protect Nicola from their ministrations and meddling.

Nicola didn't need doing over or dollying up. As far as he was concerned, she was perfect the way she was. She was brilliant with his kids. She made them laugh but, more importantly, she made them feel secure.

And she kissed like an angel. Like a bad, *bad* angel, and just the memory of their kiss had his blood heating up.

'Darling,' his mother said, 'do give us more credit than that.'

His mother was tact personified. And, despite how much she enjoyed teasing her older brother, so was Dee. They were kind, generous women. They wouldn't do anything to make Nicola feel bad about herself.

He shoved his hands into his pockets. 'Sorry. I didn't mean to suggest… It's just she's been so good for Ella and Holly. I owe her for that.'

His mother nodded her understanding. Dee bit her lip. Harry set her knife down and threw him a challenge. 'You know she still uses that blasted gym each afternoon when she puts the kiddies down for a nap.'

He stiffened. Then he set his shoulders. 'I'll think of something,' he promised. He'd find something else in the exercise line she'd enjoy more.

'In the meantime, we have this afternoon taken care of,' Dee said, rubbing her hands together. 'What fun!'

He glanced around at the three women and a grin full of reluctant admiration tugged at his lips. 'I should've known I could count on you guys.'

CHAPTER FIVE

AT LUNCH, remembering Cade's words from the previous evening, Nicola made an effort to be friendlier. Poised, self-sufficient and self-possessed was the image she wanted to portray, not stiff, standoffish and unapproachable.

'Mum,' Dee said towards the end of the meal, 'I was hoping you'd give me a haircut this afternoon for old time's sake, and I'll set your hair for you.'

'A girls' afternoon, darling? Ooh, what fun.'

Unbidden, pain pierced Nicola's chest, so sharp it almost made her double over. She swallowed back a gasp and lifted Holly out of her high chair to cuddle the child on her lap. The pain shifted and settled in her side like a stitch. She and Diane once had regular girls' nights. They'd slather on face masks and paint each other's nails. Sometimes they'd colour each other's hair. They'd play their music too loud and share their dreams and plans for the future.

They hadn't had one of those sessions in over six months and it was only now Nicola realised how much she'd missed them. She closed her eyes. Diane was still a dear friend. Maybe when Nicola returned home...

Nausea swirled through her. Diane had listened to all of Nicola's dreams for the future with Brad. She'd known how much Nicola had yearned for a home and family.

She'd known all the hopes Nicola had pinned on Brad. And yet she'd still…

Nicola buried her face in Holly's hair. There wouldn't be any more girls' days. She didn't want to hear about Diane's plans for the future with Brad. She wasn't sure she could stand it.

She shook herself, bounced Holly up and down until the child giggled. She would get over this. She would! In the interests of saving an important friendship. First, though, she needed to put a protective barrier around her heart so she would be able to bear it.

She concentrated on her breathing. Eventually she wouldn't mind hearing Diane talk about Brad. One day she wouldn't think twice about seeing them together. One day the sense of betrayal that could still turn her days dark would drain away, leaving nothing more than a faint mark.

She just wished that day would hurry up and arrive.

'Nicola, darling?'

She snapped to and found Verity smiling at her. She made herself smile back. 'Yes?'

'My darling girl, I would just love to get my hands on your hair.'

She would? She touched a self-conscious hand to her hair. These days she just washed it and pulled it back into a ponytail. No fuss. No frills. She suddenly realised she hadn't been near a hairdresser in over four months.

'Mum is magic with hair,' Dee said.

There was no denying that Verity was a very stylish woman. So was Dee, just in a younger, more relaxed way.

'Take it out of its band for a moment,' Verity ordered.

She complied. Holly laughed and reached for it. Nicola distracted her with a napkin. Shredded paper was a whole lot less painful than pulled hair.

Verity studied Nicola for a long moment. 'Hmm…'

Nicola forced herself not to fidget under that gaze, but it occurred to her that she must seem such a frump to these two lovely women. She glanced at Harry for solidarity. Harry's hair and skin glowed with good health, but the housekeeper was totally unconcerned with her appearance.

Harry shook her head. 'There's no denying that Verity has a way with these things. But listen you two…' She pointed a finger at Verity and Dee. 'Our Nic isn't the fussy sort. She won't want to spend half an hour each morning blow-drying and straightening or curling or any of that other nonsense.'

Lord, no!

And then she realised that Harry had called her 'our Nic' and her eyes filled. For a moment she felt as if she belonged.

Verity gave a sudden nod. 'I would take two to three inches off so your hair sat just above your collarbone and I'd layer it to give it some body and movement.' She tapped a finger to her lips. 'And I'd put in a long side fringe. I think it would really make the most of your beautiful eyes.'

'Ooh, yes!' Dee practically danced in her seat. 'It'd be long enough to still pull back because, whatever anyone says, it's hellishly hot out here. Ooh, ooh!' She danced in her seat some more. Her enthusiasm made Nicola laugh. 'You could scrunch dry it with a bit of mousse and I bet it'd go deliciously curly.'

'Or, if you wanted, you could blow-dry it for a more formal look,' Verity said.

'And I think some light streaks through the crown.'

'That would be lovely.'

Dee grinned. 'What do you say, Nicola? A girls' afternoon would be such fun!'

'Count me out,' Harry said promptly.

'Besides,' Dee added, 'you deserve a treat. Since we

arrived you've taken the boys under your wing and I've hardly had to lift a finger. I can't tell you how much I've relished that little holiday.'

Nicola had enjoyed adding Simon and Jamie to her little group. It had been fun. They didn't need to treat her for doing her job. But...

A new haircut?

Another step towards a new her?

Ella suddenly pouted. 'You said we could make Christmas decorations this afternoon.' Simon and Jamie added their protests too.

Nicola pulled her hair back into its ponytail. No matter how alluring the vision of female friendship and a new image promised to be, she was here first and foremost as a nanny. 'So I did. And I never break a promise.'

Dee grinned at her niece. 'I'll make a deal with you, Ella. You get Nicola for the next hour and then...' She glanced at Harry.

'And then I'll drag the paddling pool out and you can all have a splash about,' the older woman announced.

A cheer went up from Ella, Simon and Jamie. Holly bounced, threw her shredded napkin in the air and sent Nicola a toothy grin. Nicola couldn't help but smile back with her whole heart.

Cade promptly pushed away from the opposite side of the table, a dazed expression on his face. She'd been aware of him the entire meal, but had done her very best to ignore him. The memory of last night's kiss was still too vivid... and far too compelling.

'Is that okay with you, Cade?' she asked as something midway between a scowl and a grimace shadowed his face. Maybe he'd wanted to do something with Ella and Holly this afternoon and had needed her assistance, or—

He shook his head. 'I should've left ten minutes ago

when haircuts and stuff came up. Secret women's business,' he muttered. 'I've got work to do.'

'Before you go, darling, we're all dressing up tonight and eating in the dining room.'

'Fine. Whatever.' He rolled his eyes in Nicola's direction. 'My mother loves to dress up for dinner. She'd have us do it every night if she could.'

'But while I'm here I content myself with once or twice a week,' Verity said with a sweet smile. 'You don't mind, do you, Nicola?'

She was to be included? She remembered the deal she'd made with Cade. 'Not at all.'

'I think it's nice for Ella and Holly. I don't want them growing up into barbarian tomboys. I hope they can out-ride, out-muster and out-run every male on the property, but I want them to have nice manners while they're doing it. And while it might be seven hundred kilometres to the nearest shopping mall, that doesn't mean they should be deprived of the delights of nice clothes and dressing up.'

'Don't worry, Mum—' Cade dropped a kiss to the top of Verity's head '—for as long as you're around, you have a more than willing disciple in my avaricious eldest daughter.'

As if she knew he was talking about her, Ella lifted her big blue eyes and said, 'I'm wearing my yellow dress tonight.'

'And you'll look like a princess,' he informed her.

Nicola bit her lip. What on earth was she going to wear?

Cade seized the last sandwich and headed for the back door. He turned as he pushed it open. 'But in return for such a generous display of male tolerance, I want to enlist everyone's help in putting up the Christmas lights tomorrow afternoon.'

'Of course, darling,' his mother said.

'Not getting me up a ladder,' Harry muttered.

'Do we have lots of lights, Daddy?' Ella asked, her face glowing with excitement.

'Trillions,' he assured her, his eyes suddenly twinkling as they met Nicola's for the briefest of moments. And then he was gone.

Nicola, Verity and Dee spent the afternoon primping and preening. Dee set Verity's hair in hot rollers. Verity coloured Dee's hair and while the timer was set for the colour to take, she cut Nicola's hair. Unlike at a hairdressing salon, there was no large mirror for Nicola to watch and marvel as the deed was done. Instead, she sat on a chair on the shady side of the veranda, a towel firmly clasped at her throat, while Verity snipped away.

She was aware of an enormous amount of hair falling to the ground. She swallowed as a particularly long strand caught on her arm. Oh, good Lord, how much was Verity cutting off? She'd be bald!

She was aware of a growing sense of lightness. She didn't know if she liked it or not.

'There, all done.' Verity moved in front of her, lifting Nicola's chin with one finger to survey her with a critical eye. 'Perfect! Now, don't look down to see how much is gone. It'll only make your stomach clench with nerves. It's lovely, trust me.'

Nicola didn't have much choice but to do exactly that. It was far too late to put the hair back. But she couldn't help glancing down at the hair that had collected around her all the same and, as Verity had predicted, her stomach clenched.

The older woman swept the hair off the edge of the veranda and into the garden below. 'It's wonderful for the roses,' she confided.

Nicola didn't bother telling her she was sweeping them into the agapanthus rather than the roses.

Verity and Dee wouldn't let her look in the mirror when they returned to Verity's suite of rooms with its enormous bathroom. Verity put highlights in her hair and Nicola's stomach clenched even tighter. What if they turned out brassy orange or some shade of ghastly? She wanted a new image, she hungered for a new image, but...

What if, after all this work, she still looked like an overweight frump? What if she couldn't change? What if she really was a failure and a doormat and—?

Her stomach swirled. Bile rose in her throat. To take her mind off her doubts, she painted Dee and Verity's nails. Dee chose hot pink. Verity chose scarlet. Nicola painted her own nails gold. It seemed...Christmassy. And she had a deal to keep.

They talked fashion. Nicola confessed to having packed only one nice dress and a pair of black trousers that, at a pinch, she could dress up.

Dee's laptop was promptly brought out and Nicola was introduced to the joys of online shopping. She ordered clothes she'd have never bought except for Dee and Verity's urgings, their pronouncements that this top or that skirt or dress would be perfect for her. They were both so stylish and the clothes were oh-so-pretty that Nicola gulped and decided to trust them. By the time they were finished she was several hundred dollars poorer.

'They'll be here within a week,' Dee said, rubbing her hands together.

Oh, good Lord, what had she done?

With a defiant toss of her head, she unclenched her hands and relaxed her shoulders. She didn't have a wedding to pay for any more and a girl was entitled to the occasional treat, right? Dee and Verity didn't look the least bit guilty and they'd spent as much money as she had. It wouldn't hurt her to emulate them a bit more.

Poised, confident, self-possessed. She repeated the litany silently to herself as her hair was rinsed and blow-dried.

Verity stepped back with a wide smile. 'Okay, darling, time for the grand unveiling.'

Nicola's stomach immediately cramped. She did her best to keep the voice in her head, the voice so like her mother's, which criticized and nagged and told her she'd never measure up, quiet as Verity and Dee led her to a mirror.

She lowered her eyes, dragged in a deep breath and then forced her gaze upwards.

Her jaw dropped.

She lifted a hand to touch her hair.

Her eyes filled with tears. 'You've made me look pretty,' she whispered.

'Darling.' Verity put an arm around her shoulders and squeezed, beaming at her in the mirror. 'You are beautiful. And you were before all of this.'

No, she hadn't been pretty before. But now…

She couldn't believe the transformation. Her chestnut hair was sleek and shiny, the lighter highlights bringing out the colour of her eyes and complementing her skin tone.

When she shook her head, her hair swished about her in a light and flirty perfumed cloud. 'You're a magician!'

'Nonsense, you were just hiding yourself behind all that hair, that's all. It's lovely to see your face.'

You'll never be the kind of woman to turn a man's head, Nicola Ann.

She lifted her chin. *I beg to differ, Mum.*

Would she turn Cade's head?

'In the same way,' Dee added, 'you hide that lovely figure of yours beneath clothes that are much too baggy.'

That snapped her to. 'Lovely figure?' It took a concerted effort not to snort. *Dignified. Friendly and dignified.* 'I am way too curvy.' Fat. 'I need to lose at least ten kilos.'

'Nonsense!' Verity said crisply. 'You're perfect. You have gorgeous curves. I miss my curves.' She ran her hands down her sides from bust to hip. 'I seem to be shrinking as I get older.

'But you look lovely,' Nicola blurted out.

'The secret is good foundation garments.' Verity's eyes twinkled and Nicola couldn't help but laugh. 'Besides, I firmly believe that men who only like stick insects have an innate hatred of women. I, for one, have never been the slightest bit interested in pleasing them. My darling Scott, Cade and Dee's father, liked a full womanly figure. He was a big admirer of Marilyn Monroe and Jane Russell. He'd have hated all of this obsession with being skinny.' Her eyes twinkled again. 'And I'm pleased to say his son takes after him.'

Nicola blinked. Heavens, Verity didn't think there was anything going on between her and Cade, did she? She opened her mouth to disabuse her of any such notion, but Verity swung her back to the mirror. 'Dee has a dress that would look perfect on you. It'd nip you in at the waist and give you the perfect hourglass outline.'

'Ooh, yes, the cherry-red. It'd look fabulous with your hair too. You must wear it tonight. Such a transformation deserves a proper celebration.'

Nicola had to blink back tears as she suddenly realised female solidarity wasn't dead. It was alive and thriving in the world. She turned from the mirror to face the two women. 'Thank you,' she said simply with a smile from the heart.

When Nicola walked into the dining room that evening, Cade's eyes widened. The world tilted to one side and he had to brace his legs to keep his balance. The woman had killer curves!

Femme fatale. The words thumped through him, punching him in the solar plexus and emptying his lungs of air. Femme fatale had been the furthest thought from his head when she'd climbed out of the plane earlier in the month, but now...

He shook himself. He had to stop from lingering on the way her dress hugged her body. He had to get his mind off those curves—well and truly off them or he'd embarrass himself.

Farm business. Think farm business! Calving, branding, mustering...riding in all the wildness of Waminda Downs with nothing but scrub and rock and the line of the hills in the distance...the curvaceous line of those hills and—

He shook his head in an attempt to snap out of the fog he'd descended into. To one side his mother and sister beamed at him and the tie he'd donned for dinner tightened around his throat. Colour flooded Nicola's cheeks and her gaze darted away as if she was embarrassed or afraid of what he might say. She fussed about, placing Holly in her high chair and helping Ella into her seat. A strange tenderness filled him then, helping him to chain his rampant desires back under control. 'Nicola?'

She glanced up and he took his time surveying her new hairstyle. His mother and Dee hadn't ruined her, and they hadn't turned her into a plastic version of herself. They'd somehow managed to reveal the beautiful woman who had been posing as an ordinary girl for far too long.

She stole his breath.

'You look beautiful.'

She smiled then—that smile that could bowl a man over. 'Thank you.'

She bowled him over the next morning too—even though she'd returned to her usual attire of long cotton shorts and a baggy T-shirt as she and the children painted Santa pictures.

But he knew the curves that hid beneath her clothes now. He could picture them in his mind. And if she let him kiss her again—

He snapped that thought off and went to break in a brand new colt—a far more constructive outlet for his energy. He wasn't kissing Nicola again. She might kiss like a temptress. She might look like a temptress. But neither one of them needed the complication.

If he could just get the thought out of his head.

That thought was still there that afternoon, though, when he assembled everyone to help unwind and test the various strings of fairy lights. Her curves were hidden. Her new hairstyle was too because, at some stage during the day, she'd succumbed to the heat and had pulled it up onto the top of her head. But the most beguiling wisps found their way out of the knot to curl about her neck and ears.

Pretty ears.

And a neck a man would love to explore with long, slow kisses and—

Get a grip, damn it, man!

He tried not to look at her too much when he was on

the ladder and she handed him up row upon row of fairy lights to attach to the frame of the homestead.

He kept his eyes averted from her that evening after dinner too when it was time for the grand unveiling. When, at the flick of a switch, the house lit up into a sparkling fairyland.

Fairy lights wound around veranda posts and along the railings. A series of fake icicles hung from the veranda ceiling. Each door and window frame had its own set of lights. So did the shrubs and trees in the garden. Everything winked and twinkled and sparkled. Beside Jamie and Simon, Ella jumped up and down. From her spot in Nicola's arms, Holly's eyes went wide and her mouth formed a perfect O. His heart expanded and his shoulders loosened. This—all of it—was for Ella and Holly. He wasn't going to let anything, not even hormones, get in the way of that.

His smile slipped when he heard Dee murmur to their mother, 'It's a bit over the top, don't you think? I mean, an entire generator to power fairy lights?'

'Oh, I don't know,' Nicola chimed in. 'The kids just love it and it really does look pretty. Ella, Jamie and Simon are gobsmacked and will probably talk about this for years to come.'

'You're probably right,' Dee laughed. 'On his own head be it, though, because I believe he's just started a new family tradition.'

'If so, it's a lovely one,' Verity said. 'Nicola is right. It looks magical.'

'What do you think, kids?' Nicola asked. 'Should there be Christmas lights like this every year at Waminda Downs?'

A resounding cheer went up from all the children, and Cade knew then that Nicola would do everything in her power to keep her side of the bargain—to make this Christmas the best one yet. He meant to keep his word too, but… What excuse could he come up with tomorrow to keep her away from that darn treadmill? He'd run out of fairy lights.

He churned the problem over and slowly a grin spread through him. She might have an angel's own smile but, beneath it, every now and again he'd caught glimpses of a red-hot anger. He didn't condemn her for it. He understood it.

And he knew exactly where to channel it.

'Not a chance, lady.'

The voice whipped out from the shade of the corridor as Nicola reached for the door handle of the home gym. She jumped, spun and then pressed her back to the wall and clutched her chest. 'Cade!'

She tried to catch her breath. Not always easy around Cade and his watchful blue eyes. 'Do you make a habit of sneaking up on a body like that?'

Those eyes twinkled. 'Well, it's got to be said—nice body.' His glance was almost a caress. Her legs went soft and rubbery. 'But I didn't sneak up. I've been waiting here for you.'

She moistened her lips. 'Why?'

'Because a little bird told me that most afternoons when you put the children down for a nap, you head on straight down here.'

'Do you mind?' Maybe he'd had second thoughts about letting her use his ex-wife's equipment. Maybe he wanted to keep the ghosts from his past quiet. Maybe he wanted to simply keep that door closed for good.

'I don't mind at all.'

She scratched her head. 'Did you want me to help put

up more Christmas lights or something?' She brightened at that thought. Climbing ladders would be far more preferable to a stint on a rowing machine.

He leaned against the wall opposite, arms folded, and somehow it only emphasized the breadth of his shoulders. 'Be honest. Do you enjoy using the gym?'

'Enjoy?' She snorted before she could successfully remind herself that *snorting is for pigs, Nicola Ann.* 'Look, I thought we'd established that me and exercise were never going to enjoy each other's company.'

'You enjoy riding.'

'That's not exercise. Well,' she amended, 'it probably is for Scarlett, but not for me. It's fun.'

'It tones and strengthens thigh and calf muscles and it improves balance. Of course it's exercise.'

She tapped the gym door. 'I may not like it, but this is doing me good. I can run for ten straight minutes at six point five kilometres per hour on the treadmill now. I could barely manage three minutes when I started.'

'And the rowing machine?'

Her lip curled. She hated the rowing machine. Oh, who was she trying to kid? She hated that entire gym, but no pain…

'I thought you might like to give something else a try.'

'Like?'

His mouth curled up. 'Don't trust me, huh? I'm the guy that got you hooked on riding, remember?'

He was also the guy who'd kissed her with a thoroughness that still had her waking up in the middle of the night. A whole host of images assaulted her—a whole variety of ways to get some additional exercise.

She backed up a step, pointed down the corridor behind her. 'I'm nearby if one of the children wakes up.'

'I asked Dee to keep an ear out for them over the next

hour.' He frowned suddenly. 'I don't want you becoming Dee's drudge. Those boys are a handful.'

She snorted again. And then winced. She really had to get better at curbing that habit. 'They're great fun and I am in no danger of becoming a drudge. Lord, your mother, sister and housekeeper all help so much with the children that some days I feel I'm hardly pulling my weight.'

He snorted in the exact same fashion. She couldn't help noticing that he didn't sound like a pig. 'Not pulling your weight? You keep everything running like clockwork. It'd all be a shambles if you weren't here.' He sobered. 'It's been a long time since I've seen Ella and Holly so carefree and excited. I'm glad you came to stay.'

At his words, her chin lifted and her shoulders went back. She had to blink hard a couple of times. 'I'm glad I came to stay too.'

'Does that mean you're willing to risk life and limb to try out a new form of exercise?'

She gave in. The siren call of the rowing machine just wasn't loud enough. It couldn't compete with Cade's grin... or her own curiosity.

Without another word, she nodded and followed him.

A few moments later they stood in a cleared space in the barn. When Cade held out a pair of boxing gloves to her, she frowned, blinked and then put her hands behind her back. 'No way.'

'These are boxing gloves, Nicola,' he started patiently.

'I know what they are. And I repeat, no way.'

He stared at her with pursed lips.

'I've seen *Rocky*.' She hitched up her chin. 'I saw what happened to some of those guys in the ring, and they were fit! There's no way on God's green I'm going to let you hit me, regardless of what tripe you give me about how soft those gloves are. So I repeat, no way.'

He grinned so suddenly the impact was nearly physical. She planted her feet in an effort to counter it.

'I won't be hitting you, Nicola. You'll be hitting me.' He smirked. 'Or at least trying to.'

Her eyes narrowed at that. She hauled her hands from behind her back and took the gloves. He smirked again, insufferably superior, as she pulled them on. 'It's just possible that I may grow to enjoy this as much as riding Scarlett,' she warned him.

'I'm counting on it,' he said, sliding his hands into thick square mitts that had even more padding than her gloves.

'Ah, so you won't be wholly unprotected, then?'

'Nope, which is just as well when the woman I'm about to face has such a martial light in her eye.'

That made her laugh. When he squared up to her and ordered her to show him what she had, though, she found it curiously difficult to do as he asked.

He lowered his protective mitts. 'What's wrong?'

'It just seems wrong to hit you. Terribly impolite and… well, violent.'

'Pretend I'm that rowing machine.' He squared up again. 'Hit me in the middle of my left mitt.'

She did.

He lowered his hands and glared. 'Put some oomph into it!'

'I don't want to hurt you.'

'Honey, that'll be the day.'

That patronising 'honey' set her teeth on edge.

'Boxing, when it's done right, is an excellent cardio-vascular workout. And it's a good way of getting rid of pent-up tension.'

'I don't have any pent-up tension,' she managed between gritted teeth.

'Really?' His eyes narrowed. 'What did your mother

say when you told her you were coming out here for Christmas?'

Run away, Nicola Ann, with your tail between your legs, but the mess will still be here when you come back.

She let fly with a punch that thwacked satisfyingly into Cade's left mitt.

He raised an eyebrow. 'And I've been wanting to know…'

'Yes?' she ground out.

'If you've come up with a strategy for the cruel remarks that'll be headed your way at the wedding?'

Thwack! Thwack! 'What comments?'

He assumed a mocking high-pitched voice. 'You're putting on a very brave face, dear, but I can imagine how you're really feeling.'

Thwack! Thwack! Thwack!

'Put some feeling into it,' he ordered. 'Put your whole body behind it.'

Her whole body, huh?

He lifted his chin and assumed that voice again. 'This wedding must be a nightmare for you, I know, but even you have to admit that the bride is glowing. They look so happy together, don't you think?'

Thwack!

'I bet you fifty bucks that Diane throws the bouquet to you.'

She paled at that one. Thwack!

'Don't worry,' he simpered in that high-pitched voice again, 'I expect Brad will two-time her too.'

'Stop it!' she croaked. 'Stop saying such cruel things.'

'It's what people will say.' He lowered his mitts.

'And you think I'm so pathetic that I won't be able to cope with it or defend myself?'

'I think you ought to be prepared, that's all.' His eyes

suddenly flashed and his hands came back up. 'But while we're on the subject, I think your ex is a two-timing, cheating scumbag and your best friend a back-stabbing witch!'

Nicola wasn't even aware that she'd thrown the punch until it connected with Cade's jaw and sent him sprawling to the ground.

CHAPTER SIX

NICOLA stared at Cade, sprawled at her feet and with a little cry she shook off her boxing gloves and knelt in the dirt beside him, wrung her hands before touching his face. 'Oh, my God! Did I hurt you? Cade?'

Those blue eyes, normally so piercing, stared up at her, slightly dazed.

She'd meant to throw that punch, but she'd thought… Well, she'd thought he'd block it!

She swallowed. Who'd have thought she had such lightning reflexes? That punch had been fast…and…um…hard. *Put your whole body behind it.* Oh, she'd done that.

Nausea swirled through her. She'd thought he'd block her punch, but that didn't change the fact that she'd lashed out in anger.

'Cade?'

He didn't speak. Guilt, regret and remorse pounded through her and, before she could think better of it, she pressed her lips to his in an effort to take away the pain, to communicate her remorse and apologise.

He smelled of dust and sweat and horses, which should have turned her off, only it didn't. His lips were an intriguing combination of firmness and softness and they parted slightly as if he meant to deepen the kiss. Then he froze and his hands came up, gripped her arms and pushed her back as he sat up. 'What do you think you're doing? Kissing me better?'

His scorn almost scorched the flesh from her bones. 'I...'

'I'm not a child, Nicola.'

It was too much. His anger... Her guilt and remorse. That final punch had torn the lid off the emotions she'd bottled up for the last three months. She tugged herself out of his grip and stumbled blindly across to a wooden crate and collapsed on top of it, her back to Cade as she tried to tamp down on the pain and numbing sense of loss that cut deep inside her, but now that it was freed it seemed to grow in both volume and intensity.

She'd punched Cade in anger!

And then she'd kissed him. What on earth had she been thinking? The expression on his face...

I think your ex is a two-timing cheating scumbag and your best friend is a back-stabbing witch.

The words ripped off the poorly formed scab she'd tried to place over her heart and, try as she might, she couldn't control the sudden shaking of her shoulders or the silent sobs that clawed free from her chest or the tears that scorched her cheeks as her body tried to find a way to lance the poison that tangled her in knotted torment. Dropping her head to her hands, she could do nothing but give into it.

Somewhere, in a dim place of her consciousness, she was aware of embarrassment and her mother's scornful voice. *Nicola Ann, pull yourself together! You're not a child any more. What a display! You're making a spectacle of yourself.* But none of it had any effect. It didn't stop the shaking and the sobs. It didn't help the pain.

An arm went about her. Her face was pressed against the thick scratchy cotton of a work shirt encasing a warm chest that smelt of dirt and sweat and horse. A hand rubbed her back and a rich voice murmured words that didn't make sense except for their rhythm and depth, and very slowly the pressure in her chest abated. The shaking of her shoulders slowed. The sobs eased and the tears dried.

She remained where she was, drawing as much comfort and strength as she could until the internal voices grew too loud to ignore and she finally drew back, scrubbing her hands across her face in an effort to erase the traces of her tears. She didn't dare glance at Cade. Instinct told her his expression would score her too-vulnerable-at-the-moment heart, and she refused to cry again today. She'd need more deep breaths before she could face that.

'I went too far.' His voice broke the afternoon silence. 'The thing is...' he drew in a shaky breath '...I wanted to insult Brad and Diane. I don't know them and I have no right to say anything, but I am so dirty with them for what they've done to you. Nobody deserves what they did. Especially not someone like you, Nicola.'

She had to look at him and he gave her a rueful half smile and it didn't make her flinch or cringe. It helped her lift her chin and push her shoulders back a fraction.

'I think,' he continued, 'you would be a great friend to have. And I think you were probably a lovely fiancé, and you sure as hell didn't deserve what Brad and Diane did.'

His words put strength back into her spine. 'No more than you deserved what Fran dished out to you.' She moistened her lips and glanced down at her hands. 'I'm sorry I hit you. Did I hurt you?'

He shook his head. 'I wasn't expecting it, that's all. But I deserved it. I was deliberately trying to rile you. You thought I was going to block it.'

'I wasn't thinking at all, that's the problem. I just lashed out.'

They were both silent for a moment. She moistened her lips again. 'Why were you trying to make me angry?'

One of his shoulders lifted. 'I sensed you might need to vent some of your anger. I remember how angry I was in the months after Fran left and…' He shrugged again. 'I thought boxing would be more constructive than a tread-mill.' He eyed her for a moment. 'It seems to me you've been bottling a lot of stuff up. It's not healthy.'

'I didn't mean to. I…' She rested her elbows on her knees and dragged her hands back through her hair. 'It's just that my two closest confidants were Diane and Brad, and they weren't exactly available. And there was no way I was going to confide in my mother.'

'What about your other friends?'

'I didn't want to cause a big rift among our set. I didn't want people feeling they had to take sides.' She straightened. 'And the honest truth is, I don't want to lose Diane and Brad as friends. I really don't.'

Behind the blue of his eyes she could see his mind race, but he said nothing.

'Diane and I go all the way back to our first day of school. Her family have been there for me all my life. They were a haven for me when my father died, and whenever my mother became too much, and…and just everything! I can't turn my back on all that history just because she fell in love with Brad.'

'That doesn't mean you can't acknowledge your pain or your anger. If she values your friendship as much as you do, then it will survive that.'

'And if she doesn't?' She spoke her real fear out loud for the first time.

Cade didn't say anything, but she could read the answer in his eyes—if their friendship couldn't survive her honesty, then it wasn't worth saving.

She leapt up and started to pace. Gripping her hands together, she swung back to Cade. 'You know, I could've dealt with all of this so much better if they'd just been honest with me from the get-go. Instead, they kept meeting up behind my back for months before Diane eventually confessed what had happened. Brad didn't even have the courage to show his face that evening.' She flung an arm out and then started to pace again. 'I know they didn't want to hurt me, I truly believe that, but to let it all go on for so long without telling me...'

She folded her arms and paced harder, faster. 'That made me angry. That made me feel like a fool, like an idiot they didn't have any respect for. I...' She gripped her upper arms. 'I kept wondering what on earth I'd done wrong, how had I managed to so spectacularly alienate them. Had I neglected them? Had I not picked up on key signals? I mean, Diane told me that I had always been too needy and that she felt pressured, but...' She swallowed and lifted her chin. 'I didn't do anything wrong, did I?'

Cade shot to his feet. 'Hell, no!' He cupped her face in his hands. 'You didn't do one damn thing wrong.'

His eyes blazed with a ferocity, an intensity that did her soul and her confidence no end of good. 'Oh, hell, Cade.'

His eyes narrowed. 'What?'

'I said I'd be her bridesmaid,' she whispered.

Just for a moment his entire face went slack in shock. Very gently she disengaged herself from his hands. It seemed wiser not to get too close. Or needy. Because there had been a thread of truth in Diane's accusation, and Nicola had no intention of transferring her neediness to Cade.

'And I'm starting to think that maybe that was a crazy thing to agree to.'

He rolled his eyes. 'You think?'

She collapsed back down to the crate, her shoulders sagging. 'The thing is, we always said we'd be each other's bridesmaids—best friends forever and all that jazz, but...' She glanced across at Cade as he sat back down beside her. 'But now I don't think I can do it.' She swallowed. 'I don't want to do it.'

'Why did you say you would?'

'Because I do wish Diane and Brad well. I know I sound contradictory and conflicted, and that I'm angry and hurt.' She stared at her hands. 'But I really do hope they'll be happy. I agreed to be her bridesmaid because I wanted to prove that we could still be friends. And I thought that a show of solidarity like that would help prevent a falling-out among all our other friends.'

'And what's changed?'

She thought long and hard about that. 'I still want them to be happy, but it doesn't seem fair that I should be the one to tie myself into knots to make that happen. Their happiness is up to them, not me.'

She blinked and a weight lifted from her as she said the words—a load of guilt and pressure she hadn't even been aware that she carried.

'Anything else?'

'I can't make our friendship go back to the way it was before all this happened. No matter what I do. No matter how much I want it to.'

She pressed a hand to her chest to ease the sudden burning there, drew in a deep breath and blinked hard. When she was sure her voice was steady, she said, 'Those are the cold, hard facts, I'm afraid, and they need to be faced.' She couldn't hide from the truth any longer.

He reached out and squeezed her hand. 'I'm sorry, Nicola.'

'Me too.'

They sat like that for a moment. The shade that settled throughout the barn soothed her, as did the whickering of the horses in the nearby stable and the stamping of their feet. It reminded her that she had a ride to look forward to in the morning. A ride she could look forward to for every single day that she remained at Waminda. She might be down, but she wasn't out.

'What are you going to do?' Cade eventually asked.

'I have to let Diane know—tell her as soon as I can that I can't be her bridesmaid so she can make other arrangements.' And she couldn't do it by email from her laptop. She would have to speak to her friend. If not face to face, then at least ear to ear. 'Do you mind if I use the satellite phone this evening?'

'You're welcome to use it whenever you want.'

'Thank you.' She rose. 'I...um...I really ought to see to Ella and Holly now. But...Cade, thank you. All of this helped and I want you to know that I appreciate it.'

'You're welcome.'

She started to walk away and then stopped and turned back. 'About that kiss...'

He leaned back on his crate and a slow smile hitched up one side of his mouth. 'I lied. It sure as heck made me feel a whole lot better.' His body angled towards her in open invitation. Her eyes widened. Her mouth went dry. 'Any time you want to repeat it, you can bet that I'll be willing and able.'

She picked up the boxing gloves and hurled them at him. His laughter followed her all the way outside. She found herself grinning as she strode towards the house.

Later that evening, Cade waited for Nicola to emerge from his study. The rest of the family had decided on an early night and the house was quiet and still. Nicola pulled up short when she saw him.

He raked his gaze across her face and his heart clenched. She looked pale and worn out. 'How did it go?'

He spoke softly, using the same tone he used when handling a spirited horse that had been spooked. Nicola's shattered confidence, her self-belief, didn't need another battering, and he'd had no intention of retiring before finding out how her phone call with Diane had gone.

Her face crumpled and he held his arms open. She walked into them and he held her close—felt every breath she took as she fought for composure. He couldn't believe how right it felt to have her there.

Not that he had any intention of getting used to it—he was being a friend, that was all—but as the scent of strawberry jam drifted around him, all he could remember was the warmth of her lips as they'd touched his this afternoon, and the rush of sweetness that had stolen through him.

Long before he was ready to let her go she stepped back, forcing him to drop his arms. 'You didn't have to wait up for me.'

'Thought you could use a friend.' He held up two beers. 'And I thought you could use one of these.'

She eyed the beer hungrily. 'Bad for the diet,' she murmured.

'To hell with the diet.' He grabbed her hand and hauled her through the nearest set of French windows and outside into the almost cool of the night. Not that it was ever properly cool out here in December.

'Sit.' He pointed to the front step and handed her a beer. 'Drink and enjoy.'

A laugh gurgled out of her. 'Aye, aye, Captain.'

He planted himself on the step beside her. They cracked

their beers open at exactly the same moment, touched them in a silent toast and then drank deeply.

With a sigh, Nicola stretched her legs out and stared up at the night sky, her face pensive. He dragged his gaze from her lips and took another pull on his beer. 'So it was a bit rough, huh?'

'She cried. She accused me of wanting to ruin her big day. Once she got over the initial shock she apologised, said she understood, but...'

His beer halted halfway to his mouth. 'But?'

She glanced at him. 'It just cemented that our friendship will never be the same again.'

Her sadness tugged at the sore spaces inside him. 'Maybe not, but it doesn't mean you can't still be good friends, that you can't enjoy each other's company. It'll just be different. And I promise it will get easier with time.'

She stared at her beer. 'I guess you're right.'

From the light that spilled from the house and the light from the stars, he could see her face clearly. The plump full promise of her lips made things inside him clench up. The question that had been burning through him since she'd landed her punch this afternoon burst free from suddenly dry lips. 'What about Brad?'

She turned to him. 'What about him? I didn't speak to him, if that's what you mean.'

But had she wanted to? Had she hoped Brad might answer the phone? Did she secretly yearn that more than her friendship with Diane could be salvaged? Did she want Brad back?

Bile rose in his throat. 'Do you still love him?'

'I...I still care for him as a friend. He was a big part of my life for two years.'

'But if he came to you now and said he'd made a mistake and wanted to get back together with you, would you rush back into his arms?'

'I used to think that's what I wanted.'

'But?'

She turned those glorious eyes of hers on him and everything inside him tightened up. She opened her mouth. She closed it again. And then she blinked as if she'd just realised something stupendous. 'Heavens! It seems the sad fact of the matter is…' she tilted her beer at him in a kind of salute '…is that I miss Diane more than I miss Brad.'

He stared at her.

She stared back.

Then she snorted.

He couldn't help it. Suddenly his shoulders started to shake, and then they were both flat on their backs on the veranda laughing so hard he thought they'd wake the dead, or at the very least the rest of his family—and he knew exactly what his mother and Dee would make of this—but not even that thought could get his mirth back under control. Every time he thought he had it, she'd snigger, or he would, and they'd be off again.

Somewhere along the way her hand had found its way into his, but he didn't know if she had initiated the contact or if he had.

He remembered the way her lips had felt on his this afternoon. His lips ached. His groin ached. Damn it, even his skin ached.

Grinning, Nicola pushed up into a sitting position. All of the reserved hardness that she'd stepped off the plane with gone. He remained where he was, his grip around her hand tightening. He wanted a repeat performance of this afternoon, craved her kiss, her touch. All he'd have to do was tug and she'd fall sprawled across his chest.

He craved to taste the laughter on her lips. He hungered

to sample her sweetness once more. He ached to have the full sweet temptation of her pressed up against him.

She glanced down at him and slowly the sparkle left her eyes, the generous smile faltered and disappeared. She pulled her hand free.

Disappointment flushed through him, and something darker and more insistent. He pushed up into a sitting position too. 'Scared?' he taunted, though he knew that was hardly fair.

She tilted her head back and took another swig of her beer. 'How long is it since you've been with a woman?'

The question took him off guard. He scowled. 'That's none of your damn business.'

'And yet you're inviting me to share your bed and your body.'

'And you're going to refuse and turn me down.' He could read her as well as it seemed she could read him.

'Sleeping with me won't prove you're over Fran.'

He blinked, stiffened. What the hell...?

Her eyes flashed. 'How about you answer your own question? If Fran turned up here tomorrow and wanted to give your marriage another try, what would you do?'

He reared back as if she'd struck him. 'That's not going to happen.'

'That's the exact same answer I could've given you about Brad.'

She rose. His heart pounded. He didn't speak. Couldn't. The desire that had flooded him two seconds ago drained away.

Fran was Ella and Holly's mother. He owed them. If Fran came back, he'd owe it to his two daughters to give the marriage another shot.

But...

His hands clenched.

'Thanks for the beer, Cade. Goodnight.'

Nicola left and he couldn't even manage to croak a goodnight after her.

If Fran came back...

He slashed a hand through the air. Fran was never coming back and he could taste the bitterness of that knowledge on his tongue. Ella and Holly no longer had a mother. He'd failed them.

His hand clenched around his beer. He scowled into the night. He wouldn't fail them again, though.

He downed the rest of his beer and considered his intriguing nanny's strategic retreat. She wasn't immune to him. He'd felt it in her kiss. In both kisses they'd shared so far. He felt it in her gaze when she didn't think he was paying her any heed. It arced between them, unspoken, whenever their eyes locked.

He shook his head. Nicola was wrong. Things didn't have to get complicated between them. Some uncomplicated *adult* Christmas fun could be exactly what the doctor ordered. It'd provide them—him—with a much-needed release, and he'd make damn sure that it restored her confidence. Win-win.

He nodded once, hard. He had every intention of bringing Nicola around to his way of thinking as soon as he could. First, though, he'd give her some space.

Cade didn't offer to give her a boxing lesson the next afternoon. Not that Nicola expected him to. She went back to the treadmill, and to glaring at the rowing machine... and to lecturing herself.

She had to remain strong.

Sleeping with Cade... A betraying thrill shot through her. She increased the speed of the treadmill and gritted her teeth. Sleeping with Cade would undo all she'd accomplished so far. It would make a mockery of her growing sense of self-sufficiency and the realisation that she was responsible for her own happiness.

She loved her friends, she needed them, but she could rely on herself too. If she made love with Cade she would be in danger of transferring all her misplaced need to him instead of learning to stand on her own two feet first.

Developing her self-reliance and inner strength was more important than physical release and temporary pleasure.

She gritted her teeth and increased the speed of the treadmill yet again.

Nicola's eyes narrowed a couple of nights later as she watched Cade give Ella yet another sweet. She caught his eye and shook her head, but he ignored her.

They hadn't long finished a noisy game of charades and the children were buzzing and jumping, primarily due to Cade's influence. It was beyond time that they started to quieten down and get ready for bed.

He gave Ella yet another sweet. Nicola refused to let her gaze stray to the bowl of chocolate sultanas. 'You'll make her sick,' she chided.

'Nonsense! Just because you won't relax and allow yourself a few chocolate sultanas doesn't mean the rest of us have to abstain.'

'Cade!' his mother chided.

Nicola shifted on her chair. How on earth did he know about her battle with those darn sultanas?

With a giggle, Ella climbed up onto her father's lap and requested, and was given, another sweet. She grinned in triumph at Nicola.

Little monkey! But Nicola could hardly remonstrate

with her. Besides, it wasn't the child's fault but Cade's. 'Bedtime soon,' she said instead.

'Nooooo,' Ella wailed. 'Daddy, Daddy, can't we stay up a bit longer?'

She was about to tell Ella that it was already an hour after her bedtime, but Cade merely said, 'Sure, sweetheart. It's Christmastime, of course you can stay up.'

He broke into a rowdy Christmas carol. Ella promptly slid off his lap to dance with Jamie and Simon. Holly, who had started to fall asleep in Cade's other arm, promptly woke up and squealed in excitement and demanded to join in…with two sweets—one for each hand.

Nicola gritted her teeth and subsided into her chair. All of the children would be grumpy and out of sorts tomorrow. When Cade handed out more sweets and chocolates she had to get up and leave the room.

One savage tug had the refrigerator door swinging open. She seized a jug of iced water and helped herself to a glass to cool off. Cade was trying to make this Christmas memorable for his children. He wasn't flouting bedtime and mealtimes just to annoy her.

She scowled and slouched against the counter. Not that he'd be the one to deal with the fallout. He'd leave that to the hired help.

She snorted. Get over yourself, Nicola Ann. She used her mother's moniker for her. You're just grumpy because Cade has avoided you ever since that beer on the front steps.

When what you want him to do is pursue you harder.

She snapped upright. No, she didn't!

'I thought I'd find you sulking in here.'

Cade.

She turned. 'What? Have you had enough of revving the kids up for one night and now you're heading off to bed and leaving Dee, your mother and I to deal with four hyperactive children?'

'Loosen up, Nicola, and give the kids a break. It's Christmas. They're allowed to have some fun and to enjoy the season.'

'Within limits,' she shot back. 'Kids thrive on routine. Too many late nights and too many sweets will—'

'You mean that *you* thrive on routine, that *you* thrive on the safe option.'

That was when she knew they were no longer talking about the children.

'Seems to me you don't have any room in this makeover plan of yours for any spontaneity whatsoever. You stick to the plan and refuse to deviate.'

Cade was talking about what had almost happened between them and would be happening between them right now if she'd said yes instead of no the other night.

'Funny.' Her voice had gone tight and she had to swallow. 'I never picked you for a sore loser.'

The laugh he gave was harsh. 'This is about you, not me. It's about you refusing to let go and loosen up.'

She leaned forward and poked him in the chest. 'No, this is about you equating my loosening up, as you call it, with whether I'll sleep with you or not.'

'I'm not that pathetic.'

'Really?' She folded her arms. 'That night you told me you thought I needed a friend—that's the role you were playing—but you didn't really mean it, did you?' Her voice wobbled and she winced at the vulnerability that stretched through it. 'A real friend wants what's best for their friends. They don't want to see them do something that will hurt them.'

His hands clenched, his muscles stiffened and all she could think of was the way he'd held her when she'd cried, the concern in his eyes when she'd emerged from his study after her phone call to Diane.

'Look at me, Cade,' she insisted. 'I'm a mess! You're letting your frustration and your hormones override your judgement. You know all the reasons why we shouldn't...' She waved a hand to indicate what it was they shouldn't be doing. 'But you're still crazy angry with me. Well, let me plant one seriously scary picture in your mind.'

He'd gone still. She had to pause to drag in a breath. 'I might've come to the conclusion that Brad and I are better off apart, but it doesn't mean I've reconciled myself to the loss of the life I'd planned and dreamed about or to the children I dreamed of having.'

She closed her eyes against a rush of pain. When she opened them again she saw that Cade's shoulders had slumped. She had to swallow before she could continue. 'I want children so bad that some days I can't see straight. My head is not screwed on right at the moment.' She hitched up her chin. 'Say we do start an affair. What if that yearning takes me over? What if we're not as careful as we might be one time and then we're dealing with that? Do you want to be a part of that?' she asked hoarsely.

'No.'

'Me neither.'

Neither of them moved. Neither of them said a word.

'Can I put the children to bed now?' she whispered.

'Please.' He nodded, his voice as hoarse as hers.

She fled before she could do anything stupid like kiss him.

CHAPTER SEVEN

CADE jerked awake from a dead sleep. What the...?

Thump! Somebody whacked his feet. For the second time, he suspected.

'Get up, Cade.'

'Mum? What the hell...?' He struggled upright and tried to blink sleep from his eyes. His room was in complete darkness.

He clicked on the bedside light. The clock showed three a.m. He snapped into instant alertness. 'Who's ill?' He shot out of bed, pulling a T-shirt on over his head. He didn't bother with jeans over his boxers. This far from civilization, every second counted. If someone needed the Flying Doctor...

An icy hand wrapped about his heart. 'Ella? Holly?' he croaked.

Verity Hindmarsh folded her arms and glared at him. 'It's not serious but it's certainly unpleasant and of your making. So you can haul your butt out there and help that poor girl.'

He didn't wait to hear more, but shot towards the children's bedrooms. He stopped short in Ella's doorway and his heart clenched. Nicola sat on Ella's bed holding a bowl for the child as she was monumentally and comprehensively sick. There was evidence that Ella had been sick before Nicola had been able to reach her.

To make Nicola's task all the more difficult, Holly clung to her, grizzling into her neck. He could see that Holly had been sick all over herself and Nicola. Nicola's cotton nightie clung to one breast, the wet material practically transparent.

He turned his gaze away and pushed himself forward into the room. Nicola glanced up and relief lit her eyes. How long had she been struggling with this alone?

Ella lifted her head, her eyes swimming with tears, her face a picture of misery. 'Daddy, I did eat too many lollies and they made me vomit.'

Only she pronounced it 'bomit', which would normally have made him smile, except…

It's not serious, but it's…of your making.

He'd created this mess? He'd made his children sick? Bile rose in his throat as he battled a cold, hard anger with himself. There'd be plenty of time for recriminations later. Recriminations wouldn't help Ella and Holly at the moment. Or Nicola.

He swallowed. 'What can I do?'

'Holly needs to be cleaned up. Ella…'

Her eyes told him that Ella wasn't through with being sick yet.

'Holly, honey, you want to go to Daddy?'

Holly screamed and clung tighter to Nicola's neck. Ella started to cry. 'I want Daddy to stay here.'

No further communication was needed. He took Nicola's spot on the bed. She handed him a damp washcloth and a clean bowl. 'I won't be long.'

'Take the time to have a shower too,' he said softly. She deserved to be as comfortable as she could be given the situation. He predicted that with Holly in her current mood, it'd take them an age to get her back down to sleep.

She glanced down at the front of herself and her cheeks reddened. With a nod she was gone, taking Holly, the dirty bowl and her magnificent breasts with her.

He shook that last thought away and tended his daughter.

Nicola was back wearing a fresh nightie and a terry-towelling robe in less time than he dreamed possible. He frowned. 'Holly?'

'Sleeping like a baby.'

He gaped. 'But how...?'

She shrugged but her eyes danced. 'What can I say? I'm a hell of a woman.'

Her teasing lightened something inside him. She'd returned smelling all the more strongly of strawberry jam and it eased the sour smell of sickness that pervaded the room. He pulled a deep breath of it into his lungs.

'Besides, it's what you pay me for.'

'You deserve a pay rise.'

'Too many nights like this and I'll take you up on that.'

Amid all the vomit and guilt, she'd made him want to smile. He wouldn't have believed that possible. He watched her assess Ella, who was drooping.

'She needs to be bathed and her bed needs to be stripped and remade.' She quickly and deftly removed Ella's pyjamas as she spoke. 'I've run a bath and as you're stronger than me...'

He nodded and took Ella through to the bathroom and bathed her. She cried and protested, but was too tired to put up much of a fight.

When he returned to the bedroom, the bed had been made up with fresh sheets and Nicola quickly helped Ella into a cool cotton nightie. He tucked her into bed, the guilt he'd kept at bay starting to prickle and burn.

Nicola knelt down in front of Ella. 'Sweetie, I need you to take three little sips of water for me.'

'I don't want to!'

'Honey, have I ever lied to you?'

Ella shook her head.

'I promise you'll feel better if you have a little drink.'

Ella finally nodded, but she needed coaxing and cajoling every step of the way. Cade couldn't help but marvel at Nicola's combination of patience, firmness and gentleness.

'Sing me a song,' Ella demanded with a fretful squirm.

Cade wanted to order his daughter to say please, but Nicola forestalled him with a light touch on his arm. 'First Daddy has to dim the light, and then you have to lie still and close your eyes.'

''Kay.'

Cade dimmed the light and then stretched out beside Ella, his back resting against the headboard as he gently wiped her hair back from her forehead. Nicola settled on the end of the bed. She pulled in a breath and then calmly and quietly sang "Silent Night."

The soft strains of the song soothed Ella and helped ease the beast raging in Cade's own breast. He closed his eyes too and drank the song in, her voice so true it lifted the hairs on his arms.

When it was finished they sat in the quiet for a bit. Her touch on his arm had his eyes flying open. With a finger to her lips, she led him out of Ella's bedroom, the child sleeping quietly now.

With a quick smile she swooped down and picked up the soiled bed-linen and walked away with a soft 'Goodnight, Cade.'

He wouldn't sleep. Not yet. He followed her into the

kitchen, but she moved all the way through to the laundry and set a load going.

He put the kettle on and waited. 'Tea?' he offered when she reappeared.

She hesitated, her gaze sweeping across his face. Finally she nodded. 'Something herbal would be nice.'

He made them mugs of peppermint tea, even though he didn't like the stuff. Penance, he told himself.

'I'm sorry about that,' he murmured once they were both seated. 'You tried to warn me that too many sweets would make them sick. I didn't listen.'

She shrugged. 'We live and learn. Don't beat yourself up about it.'

Don't beat himself up? He shot to his feet. 'I made them sick! I'm supposed to protect them and look after them and...'

Her eyes widened.

'I want to make Christmas special for them, but...damn it, I'm making a hash of everything! Those poor kids.' He fell back into his chair. 'They drew the short straw in the parents stakes, no mistake about it, and...' He couldn't go on. His throat had grown too tight.

'Now where did I put that hair shirt?' Nicola said with an efficient crispness so utterly devoid of sympathy it made him sit back in shock.

'Stop being such a martyr.'

Martyr? Him?

'I'm going to tell you a hard truth.' She leaned towards him, her voice still crisp, but her eyes incredibly gentle and soft. 'It doesn't matter how fabulous you make this Christmas, it doesn't matter how many fairy lights you put up or how many sweets and chocolates you stock up on or how many presents you buy them, it will never make up to them for not having their mother. Furthermore,' she added when he opened his mouth, 'you will never be able to make that up to them. Ever. No matter what you do.'

The truth of her words had the fight whooshing out of him. He ached to make it up to Ella and Holly, wanted to so badly—needed to—but...

He closed his eyes.

'Cade?'

He opened them again. The softness, tenderness, in her eyes belied the hard truths she'd uttered.

'Stop fighting a losing game and just focus on ensuring they feel secure in your love. Do what you've been doing—be fully involved in their lives, surround them with their extended family at every opportunity, and create a community here at Waminda Downs that they can rely on.'

'There has to be more that I can do!' He wanted there to be more that he could do.

'There is.'

He glanced up.

'You can stop punishing yourself for what happened between you and Fran. How are you going to help Ella and Holly come to terms with their mother's desertion if you haven't come to terms with it yourself?'

He had no answer to that. He wanted to rant and rail and break things, but Nicola didn't deserve that.

'But I can tell you that having one parent who is completely invested in your life is far better than two parents who are distant and critical. Ella and Holly at least have that.'

Too right! He was a hundred per cent behind his kids, but his heart burned as he gazed into Nicola's eyes and the shadows there. She obviously knew what she was talking about. No wonder she'd made a family from her friends. No wonder Diane and Brad's betrayal had rocked the foundations of her world and all she held dear.

'Ella and Holly are lucky in lots of ways.'

He forced himself to consider her words seriously, and for the first time in a very long time he recognised their truth. 'They're healthy,' he said slowly, and then grimaced. 'At least, as a general rule they're healthy.' He paused. 'They have a grandmother, an aunt and cousins who adore them. And…and Waminda is a great place to live.'

'And they have you,' she said with a warmth that engulfed him. 'You should take a lot of heart from the fact that Ella is so well adjusted. Fran's leaving would have been traumatic for her, but she's a happy, stable little girl. She's not too clingy, isn't waking up in the middle of the night screaming with nightmares, and she doesn't constantly worry where you are.'

'We've been through all that,' he admitted.

'It seems to me she's over the worst of it now.'

Nicola was right. He nodded. 'This single parent gig isn't easy. Half the time I don't seem to know what I'm doing. And the rest of the time I simply feel clueless, but…' He rubbed a hand across his jaw. 'Maybe I should have more faith in Ella and Holly.'

'And yourself.'

He met her gaze. 'Thank you.' He meant it.

Nicola smiled back, but her gaze had dropped to his lips and he could read the hunger that raced across her face. The same hunger surged through him.

She snapped away, and then rose and rinsed her mug. 'I'm off to bed.' She turned in the doorway. 'Would you tell Jack that I won't make my riding lesson in the morning?'

'Sure thing. You deserve a lie-in.'

She shook her head with a low laugh. 'The children are going to be out of sorts and all over the place tomorrow. I'd like to be close by in case they wake early.'

It struck him then that she'd be paying for his evening's folly for the next twenty-four hours. He wanted to apologise again, only he had a feeling she'd make another hair shirt quip or call him a drama queen.

'Goodnight, Cade.'

He settled for a ''Night, Nicola. Sleep well,' instead.

Cade winced at the dark circles under Nicola's eyes when he saw her at lunch the next day.

All the children were whingey and whiny, hard to please, and he marvelled anew at her patience and her ability to distract them and keep them semi-amiable.

'That girl is a saint,' his mother murmured.

He glanced around. 'Where's Dee?'

'Gone for a lie down. She's only had a morning of this and she's exhausted.'

He bit his lip. 'Were the boys ill too?'

'Unlike you, Dee wouldn't let them have any more sweets, so no. They're just out of routine, that's all.'

He grimaced, suitably chastened. 'I've learned my lesson,' he promised and his mother's face softened. He huffed out a breath. 'I feel bad that Nicola has to deal with the fallout when the fault was mine.'

He bit his lip and pondered his afternoon's workload. 'Will they go down for their usual nap this afternoon?'

Verity nodded. 'It'll be a battle to get them there, but once they're down they'll be out for the count. They probably won't surface for a couple of hours.'

Good. 'Would you and Dee be able to hold the fort for an hour or so, then? Nicola skipped her riding lesson this morning. I thought I might take her out this afternoon to get some fresh air into those cheeks of hers.'

'I think that's a lovely idea.'

With a nod, he grabbed a sandwich and made for the cattle yards, intent on getting his afternoon's work done in good time.

Nicola collapsed into an easy chair in the living room. 'They're down.' Finally. What a day.

'Hallelujah,' Dee murmured.

Nicola opened her eyes when she sensed Cade's presence in the room. He carried in a jug of iced water and five glasses. Slices of lemon floated in the jug and the ice chinked against its side in a cooling, welcoming symphony. He poured each of them a glass.

'I'm sorry,' he said, handing the drinks around. 'It's my fault you've all had such a difficult day.'

'It happens,' Harry said philosophically.

'Are you completely fagged?'

She blinked when she realised the question was directed at her. The short answer was yes, but...

She took one look at his face and tossed her head. 'How pathetic do you think I am? I'm fighting fit.' She emphasized the word fit. Then she grinned. 'I'm a lean, mean fighting machine.'

That hooked up one side of his mouth, enhancing a dimple she found oddly fascinating, enhancing lips she found enthralling. Need mushroomed inside her with a speed that made her hands clench.

He inserted a disc into the CD player and the strains of something soft and classical filled the room. Verity, Dee and Harry all puffed out blissful sighs and closed their eyes. He beckoned to her and she rose and followed him out of the room.

He took her now-empty glass and set it on the sink. 'I thought if you wanted...if you'd like it...we could go for a ride.'

All her tiredness fled. 'I'd love that!'

'Good. Go change and then meet me down at the stables.'

She changed into jeans and pulled on the riding boots Jack had dug out for her use, and was down at the stables in double-quick time. Cade already had Scarlett and his steed—a beautiful big bay called Ben Hur—saddled.

'Need a leg up?'

She stuck her nose in the air. 'Most certainly not.' It had taken her a while to master the skill of mounting, but in the two and a bit weeks she'd been here her legs had strengthened and grown more flexible.

When she mounted, not only without mishap but with credible grace, she could only grin down at Cade and thank the powers that be. Falling flat on her face would not have instilled in him much confidence in her riding ability and she didn't want to give him any reason whatsoever to cancel their ride. She gathered the reins in the way Jack had taught her and watched as Cade leapt up into the saddle.

Ooh, nice! She wanted to make it look that smooth and effortless. Of course, he had the advantage of long legs.

And a nice tight butt that—

Scarlett danced as Nicola's hands unconsciously tightened on the reins and she immediately relaxed them and forced her gaze from Cade's drool-inducing physique to stroke her steed's neck and murmur soothing nonsense.

Cade surveyed her and nodded in evident satisfaction. It made her warm all over. Not that she should dwell on that for too long either. 'Where are we going?' She blamed her breathlessness on the exertion of mounting and controlling her steed. Which, she admitted to herself, was too pathetic to believe, but she held tight to it all the same.

'Has Jack taken you to the canyon yet?'

Canyon? She shook her head, intrigued.

'Then that sounds as good a destination as any. C'mon.' With a jerk of his head, he headed towards the gate that led out of the home paddock.

'Let me,' she said. 'I've been practising this.'

Manoeuvring Scarlett into position as Jack had shown her, she opened the latch and swung the gate open without needing to dismount.

'Nice,' Cade remarked, closing it again once they'd passed though. He stared at her. 'Jack's right, you look as if you were born to the saddle.'

'Would you laugh at me if I told you that's how I feel too?'

'No, I'd ask you why it's taken so long for you to learn to ride when it's obviously such a passion and something you've always wanted to do.'

She pursed her lips, shrugged. 'My mother always refused to keep a horse.'

'Why?'

'She said that if I was that clumsy in ballet shoes I'd be an absolute nightmare on a horse.'

His mouth tightened. 'I get the distinct impression I wouldn't like your mother.'

Nicola gave a short laugh. 'She'd love you. You tick all the right boxes—broad shoulders, good-looking...own your own cattle station.'

'Hmph!'

They rode in silence for a while and Nicola revelled in the swaying motion of her horse and the stark beauty of the landscape and the dry dusty air.

'Why didn't you learn to ride later? Once you became an adult?'

'I...' She frowned. 'It didn't seem very practical in the city. I just kept putting it off.'

As soon as the words left her mouth she realised they

were a lie. She recalled all the resolutions she'd come out here with and hitched up her chin. 'Actually, that's not true.' She thought about it. 'I didn't bother to learn because none of my friends were interested in learning with me.' Horses made Diane shudder. 'I was too spineless to learn on my own.'

He didn't say anything for a long moment. He shifted in his saddle. 'And now?'

'Oh, now I'm hooked. And now that I know what an idiot I've been...' She frowned. 'People do keep horses in the city, don't they?'

'Sure they do.'

'I'm going to join a riding club.' There'd be one in Melbourne somewhere. 'I'm going to get my own horse.' Excitement surged through her. 'It's going to be fabulous!'

He grinned at her enthusiasm and life seemed suddenly so full of possibility she wanted to fly. 'Can we canter?' she breathed.

In answer he tossed her a grin that made her heart thud against her ribs, before he urged Ben Hur into a canter. At the touch of Nicola's heels, Scarlett surged after him, and Nicola gave herself up to the feel of the wind in her face and the exhilaration of the ride. Riding like this quietened all the voices in her head that told her she wasn't good enough, that she'd never be good enough. It allowed her to concentrate instead on feeling at one with her horse. It flooded her with strength and peace and harmony.

When Cade brought his horse to a halt, she pulled Scarlett to a halt beside him. 'Magic,' she breathed.

And then her jaw dropped.

Cade's mouth kicked up at the corners. 'This is the canyon.' He shrugged. 'In all honesty, it's more a gorge, but we have delusions of grandeur so we call it the canyon.'

'Wow!'

'It's something, isn't it?'

Something? Majestic, eternal, imposing were the words that came to mind.

The land in front of them dropped away in a series of dramatic rock shelves. The rock was baked red but deep cream and yellow veins striped through it. Water glinted in the base of the canyon. Its other side rose in a sheer cliff. Three-quarters of the way up, it curved inwards as if eroded by thousands of years of wind and sand. It looked like a giant curling wave waiting to break on a stretch of deserted beach.

The blue sky and the red rock formed a contrast that sang to her soul, though she couldn't have said why. On the other side of the canyon, the land was dotted with saltbush and the dry brown grass that the cattle roamed far and wide to graze upon. From beneath the brim of her hat, she couldn't see any cattle, but she did see a mob of kangaroo. There had to be at least twenty of them, most of them sprawled out in whatever shade they could find. A big buck stared across at them for a moment and then went back to grazing.

'It's beautiful.' The words didn't seem enough to capture the eternal grandeur of the landscape, but it was all she had to offer.

He nodded. 'In times of flood the water roars through here. There's a place to ford further downriver, which is handy when we're mustering.'

'Does it flood often?' It'd be hard being stranded out here so far from civilisation in a flood.

'There've been two decent ones in living memory, but the homestead is built on higher ground. We've never had to evacuate.'

Still…it took a special kind of person to live out here, battling drought and flood and bushfire. Cade had a grit that she admired. A grit she was determined to cultivate for herself.

'I owe you an apology.'

She barely heard him. 'Oh!' She pointed. Her mouth opened and closed. 'Emus,' she gasped out.

He chuckled. The sound was almost enough to make her drag her eyes from the five giant birds that streaked away until they were lost in the distance. She'd never seen an emu in the wild before. It shouldn't have astonished her, she supposed, but...

Lord, what a greenhorn she must seem. She turned to Cade to find him staring at her, an odd light in his eyes. Then she recalled his words. She moistened her lips. 'An apology?'

'Yeah.'

Although he wore an Akubra, he squinted in the light. Or was it that he just didn't want to meet her eye?

His gaze speared hers as if she'd asked that out loud. 'I've been acting like a jerk and I want to apologise.'

'Um...' She blinked. 'Okay.'

'The thing is...' He went back to squinting. 'I haven't been with a woman since Fran left. I haven't wanted to be with a woman.'

She swallowed. 'You've had your mind on other things. I mean, Fran's leaving must've been an enormous shock to begin with, and then there was Ella and Holly's welfare to consider. On top of all that, you're running a cattle station. It's not like you've had a lot of spare time on your hands, Cade.'

She thought back to the way he'd kissed her, to the latent power of his body, to his impressive...um...virility. Sure, their clothes had stayed on, but she'd been just about as closely pressed up against him as a body could get. She'd felt the full might of his masculinity. The memory made her mouth dry and an ache start up between her legs.

Actually, when she thought about it, Cade's abstinence was surprising. Very surprising. But it was also understandable.

His lips twisted. 'The thing is…that all changed when you showed up.'

'Liar.' She adjusted her hat. She suspected he was trying to pump up her confidence. 'There wasn't a hint of anything between us when I first climbed out of the Cessna.'

'Maybe not, but then you smiled at me.'

She had?

'I introduced you to Scarlett. You smiled…and I wanted you then and there. No preliminaries. No warning. It knocked me for six.' He scowled. 'I haven't stopped wanting you since. Kissing you only made it worse.'

Her jaw dropped.

'Look, I'm not trying to excuse my behaviour. I shouldn't have taken my frustration out on you yesterday evening. I shouldn't have pressured you to act against your better judgement. I acted like a horny teenager and I'm sorry, but I thought if you knew why I'd lost my head so completely you mightn't look on me with such a harsh eye.'

The embarrassed half-smile, half-grimace reminded her of Ella when she'd been caught out in some minor misdemeanour. It made her want to smile, but she bit the impulse back. She needed to check something before she could give into it. 'So we're back on the same page as far as…as far as sex is concerned?'

'Yep.' He nodded.

The ache between her legs intensified. She forced herself to smile. 'Okay, apology accepted.'

'Nicola?'

He forestalled her before she could turn Scarlett around and head back towards the homestead.

'I'm hoping that we can be friends. Real friends.'

Three weeks ago that word would've induced a shudder. Now?

She leaned across and held out her hand. He shook it with that firm grip that made her want to swoon. 'You have yourself a deal.'

Beneath the brim of his hat, his eyes shone out blue for a moment. 'Thank you.'

CHAPTER EIGHT

'Nic?'

'Yes, honey?'

It was Christmas Eve, dinner was long over and all the children had quietened down after a rowdy game of Trouble. Ella was sitting next to Nicola on one of the sofas, her head resting against Nicola's shoulder. The soft weight of the child and her absolute trust pierced straight into the centre of Nicola, making her wish...

She pulled in a breath and pushed the thought away. She would not allow it to mar the mood of the evening. Contentment stretched through the living room, along with expectation and hope. The atmosphere as unique to Christmas as the scent of cinnamon and mince pies.

She glanced down when Ella didn't continue with her question. 'What do you want to know, pumpkin?'

Ella chewed her lip and then climbed right into Nicola's lap. 'What if Santa doesn't come?'

She suppressed a smile. 'Why wouldn't he come?'

She shared a glance with Cade. He wore a pair of grey cargo shorts and a blue shirt that matched his eyes exactly. Holly had fallen asleep and he cradled her in his arms. The contrast between the big, tanned man—the broad shoulders and the long, strong legs—and the small child with her delicate pink-white skin and fine blonde hair, made her breath hitch and the pulse in her throat quicken. Everything about him ravished her senses. She forced her eyes back to Ella before he could see the desire that flashed in their depths.

'Well...' Ella drew out, 'Waminda is a very, very, *very* long way from Brisbane.' To her childish mind, Brisbane was the centre of the universe. 'Maybe,' she continued, 'Santa doesn't know we're here.'

'But we sent him a letter, remember?'

'Do you think he got it?'

'I'm sure of it.'

The blue eyes, so like her father's, brightened. Ella's questions, her hope, reminded Nicola of the Christmases of her own childhood—the loneliness and inevitable disappointment. She understood Ella's fear. 'And don't forget,' she whispered to the child, 'Santa is magic.'

'So he'll come?'

'Uh-huh.'

'You promise?'

'I promise.'

Her assurances seem to satisfy Ella, who snuggled into Nicola all the more securely. Cade sent Nicola such a warm smile of thanks it curled her toes.

'Nic?'

What this time? She glanced down. 'Yes?'

'Do you think Mummy will come tomorrow?'

Every adult in the room—Cade, Harry, Verity, Dee and her husband, Keith, who'd arrived earlier in the day—all stiffened. Nicola did her best to keep her body relaxed. Ella would unconsciously pick up on any tension she radiated and it would unsettle and upset her.

Was this—seeing her mother—what Ella had pinned all her Christmas hopes on? The greyness of Cade's skin, the haggard expression on his face, made her heart burn. Whatever anyone else in the room thought, she couldn't lie to Ella. If seeing her mother was the child's dearest wish, it would be hard getting her through tomorrow, but it wouldn't be as bad as giving her hope that would go unfulfilled.

She caressed the hair back from Ella's brow. 'Pumpkin, I haven't spoken to your mummy, but I don't think she'll be able to make it tomorrow.'

'The day after?'

Nicola's chest cramped. How could any woman turn her back on such a beautiful, loving child? Fran must have a heart of stone. She tried to keep her breathing steady. 'We can keep our fingers crossed, but I really don't know. I think she'd let us know if she was coming for a visit.'

She watched as Ella digested her words. 'Will you be here?'

'I promise.' She crossed her heart. 'And we're all going to have such fun tomorrow. I mean, you have your daddy and Holly here, and your grandma, Auntie Dee and Uncle Keith, not to mention Simon and Jamie, and Harry and me. That's pretty lucky, don't you think?'

Ella thought about that for a moment and then she smiled. 'Yes,' she pronounced. 'And you really, truly think Santa will come?'

'I really, truly do.'

Will you sing a Christmas carol?' Ella whispered.

Ella's favourite was *Silent Night*, so Nicola started to sing it. One by one, the other adults joined in. Before the first verse was over, Cade rose to put Holly down. By the end of the song, Keith and Dee had taken a twin apiece and Cade returned to carefully lift Ella from Nicola's arms.

'I'll be fine,' he murmured when she made to rise too.

She couldn't read his eyes, but she subsided into her seat, sensing he wanted to be alone with his daughter, to stare down at her while she slept and to give thanks for her.

Harry pushed out of her chair. 'I'm off to bed.'

'Nicola—' Verity rose '—I suspect we've seen the last of Dee and Keith for the night.'

Nicola grinned. The couple's evident delight at seeing each other after ten days apart had been all too plain.

'I also suspect that it will be a big day tomorrow.'

'I expect you're right on both counts.'

'So I'm going to retire early.'

'Sleep well.'

Verity turned in the doorway. 'I'm glad you're spending Christmas with us this year.'

She couldn't mistake the older woman's sincerity, and she had to swallow down an unexpected lump. 'Thank you. I'm glad too.'

When Cade returned, he glanced around and blinked.

She laughed. 'It seems the consensus was for turning in early.'

He collapsed on the sofa beside her. 'Fair enough.'

She stared at him for a moment. 'You okay?'

'Sure, I…'

'Ella's question about her mum was a humdinger. It seemed to hit you all for six.'

He shook his head. 'It took me off guard. God knows why. I should've expected it, I suppose, but she stopped asking about Fran months ago.'

It took an effort of will not to reach out and touch him. Every atom of her being begged her to, her mouth drying at the memory of the lean hard feel of him. Her fingers curled, her blood quickened, her lips parted to drag in a ragged breath.

He turned, his eyes flashing. 'Why the hell couldn't you just lie to her?' His hands clenched. 'Why couldn't you have left her with a tiny shard of hope?'

She flinched at his vehemence…and the direction her

thoughts had taken. Her heart pounded against her rib-cage. She dragged in a breath and tried to gather her wits. 'Do you...do you think there is any hope?' Had she read that wrong? A heavy weight settled in the pit of Nicola's stomach. Would Fran come back and claim her family?

'No!' He stabbed a finger at her. 'But that's not the point. Ella is just a child, a little girl. It was cruel to...'

Maybe it was his own hope Cade was trying to keep alive, not Ella's. A chill travelled up her backbone. Her chest throbbed. She couldn't speak.

His eyes blazed. 'You could have invented something, fibbed a little. She would've forgotten all about it tomor-row in the Christmas excitement.'

Her chin shot up. 'I will not lie to your daughter—not today, not tomorrow, not ever! I know what it's like to ache for something on Christmas Day. It's a day of miracles, right?' Her hands fisted. 'And I remember the crushing disappointment that came at day's end when I realised my wish wasn't going to come true. I will not put Ella through that. *That* would be cruel.'

His mouth opened and closed, and then he sank back against the sofa cushions and he dragged a hand down his face, swore softly. Neither of them spoke for a while. The Christmas tree twinkled benignly in the corner. 'What did you hope for?' he finally asked.

She'd expected him to continue arguing with her. His unexpected question took her back to a time of vulnerabil-ity and disappointment. It took her a moment before she could speak. 'Usually I just hoped that the spirit of the day would infect my parents and that they'd unbend enough to...to play with me.'

He stared and she found herself continuing. 'I didn't lack for presents; it was just...I was always told that I was luckier than most little girls and to go play on my own.'

She shrugged. 'One year I wished with all my might for a rowdy Christmas dinner with lots of crackers to pop and the reading out of corny jokes followed by the singing of Christmas carols.'

That hadn't happened either.

She sensed the exact moment the fight left Cade's body. She bit back a sigh. 'Look, I'm not telling you this to make you feel sorry for me. It's just that, as a child, I knew what it was like to hope for the impossible and not get it—to not even realise it was impossible in the first place. Telling Ella that her mother might show up is only setting her up for unnecessary heartbreak because, believe me, come tomorrow she won't have forgotten. She'd spend the day waiting for it to happen, waiting for her mother to walk through the door. Now, hopefully, she can focus on all the other good bits of the day instead. She might get a bit sad about her mum, but there's absolutely nothing you can do about that, Cade. No matter how much you might want to. Besides, Ella is entitled to her sadness on that count.'

He blinked as if he hadn't considered that before. He opened his mouth, closed it, and then dragged a hand down his face. 'I'm still not sure I agree with the way you handled it, but I appreciate you telling me the reason why.'

At least his anger had abated, if not his worry. She pulled in a breath. 'I think if we lie to Ella we're betraying her trust. I think if we fib to her—even with good intentions—it will lessen her faith in us.'

His jaw dropped open.

'I think fibbing to her will do more harm than good. Her faith in you, Cade, is the biggest gift you can give her. I'm pretty sure you wouldn't want to do anything that might damage that.'

'Hell, no!' He swallowed. 'I hadn't considered it from that angle.'

He didn't say anything for several long moments, but she sensed that beneath the silence his mind raced. He suddenly muttered an oath and swung to face her more fully. 'I wanted to protect Ella from more pain, but lying to her would be unforgivable. You're right. My word should be something she can trust and always rely on—not something to doubt and question.'

Nicola let out a breath.

'I'm sorry I rounded on you. You saw it all much clearer than I did.'

Her heart unclenched a fraction, and then it clenched up tighter than before. She gripped her hands together. 'Are you sure it's not your own hope you're trying to keep alive rather than Ella's?'

His head came up. 'Why the hell would I want to do that?'

'Because if Fran did show up, maybe it'd mean you weren't a failure. And that, in turn, would help ease your guilt.'

And maybe because you still love her? But she left that unsaid. She didn't have the heart for it.

'The thing is,' she continued, 'the breakdown of your marriage doesn't make you a failure. You did everything you could to save it. As far as I can see, you have absolutely nothing to be guilty about.'

He stared at her as if he didn't know what to say and it suddenly hit her that it was Christmas Eve and he'd specifically asked her for Christmas spirit and cheer. She made herself smile. 'You're a wonderful father, Cade.' She tapped her watch. 'And look, it's almost Christmas. All you can do is focus on having a lovely day tomorrow and making it special and exciting for Ella and Holly.' She nudged him with her shoulder. 'Christmas spirit, remember?'

Slowly he nodded and his shoulders went back. 'Just concentrate on the stuff I can control, right?'

He smiled then. And she had no hope whatsoever of controlling the way her heart pitter-pattered.

Or the way the breath hitched in her throat.

His gaze lowered to her mouth and his eyes darkened to a deep stormy blue. The air between them crackled with energy and electricity.

He shot off the sofa. 'Goodnight, Nicola.'

Pitter-patter. Pitter-patter. She closed her eyes. 'Goodnight, Cade.'

The next morning Nicola rose at six o'clock. A peek into Ella's room and then the boys' room confirmed they all still slept soundly. Holly would sleep through to her usual seven o'clock, but Nicola had fully expected to find the other children wide awake and bouncing off walls.

She sneaked down to the stables to give Scarlett a Christmas carrot. Jack and several of the other stockmen and jackaroos were holding their own Christmas festivities in the stockmen's quarters, so she left a box of old English toffee, that she'd discovered Jack had a fondness for, on the bench by his front door where he had his morning coffee. He should find it first thing.

She turned to make her way back to the homestead, but paused to drink in the early morning air. At this time of the day the light was clear and crisp. The landscape didn't yet shimmer with its usual heat haze, and the light was easy on the eyes. It allowed her to survey, unhindered, all the natural rugged beauty of the place before the sun blazed down with its hard blinding ferocity.

The khaki-green of the mulga scrub contrasted prettily with the yellow-white of the grass...and beneath it all the red dirt of the Outback. She hadn't expected to find so much beauty out here in the western reaches of Queensland. She hadn't fully appreciated it when she'd first arrived. But this place and its people had helped her heal and she gave thanks that she could now see and appreciate the stark and ancient grandeur of the landscape. And that she had the best part of another month in which to enjoy it.

Christmas at Waminda Downs! An optimism she hadn't allowed herself to feel for this day since she was a child welled in her now. She grinned and then set off at a trot for the homestead.

Entering her room via the French windows, the first thing Nicola saw was Ella sitting in the middle of her double bed. Her heart tripped. Had Ella panicked when she hadn't been able to find her? Had she leapt to the conclusion that, just like her mother, Nicola hadn't kept her promise and had deserted her?

'Hey, chickadee!' She swept her up in her arms for a hug and then plonked them both back down on the bed. 'Merry Christmas.'

'Merry Christmas.' A smile warred with a frown on the child's face.

'I went down to the stables to wish Scarlett a merry Christmas,' she confided.

'I thought you were in the bathroom.'

Okay, Ella hadn't been worried about her whereabouts, so...?

'Excited?' she asked.

'What if Santa didn't come?' the little girl blurted out. 'He forgot last year.'

Ah, the puzzle pieces slotted into place.

'Did you look?' Ella whispered. 'Was there anything in our stockings?'

She understood it wasn't the presents that Ella needed.

It was the magic and the hope. 'I haven't looked yet. Do you want to go and do that now?'

Ella nodded, and while she was too big to be carried much any more, Nicola knew that the child needed the security. So she lifted her up onto her hip and started towards the living room.

Then she halted.

Ella's bottom lip started to quiver, but Nicola winked at her. 'You know, I think we need your daddy for this too.' She detoured to Cade's room and knocked on his door. A muffled sound emerged that she chose to interpret as a 'what?' or a 'yes?' rather than an oath.

'Wake up, sleepy-head, the fun's about to start and you don't want to miss it.'

'Don't you dare start without me!'

There was a thump and a couple of bumps and a muffled curse or two and Ella giggled. 'Daddy's funny.'

'Hilarious,' he growled, flinging the door open and seizing Ella in his arms and swinging her around until she squealed.

His T-shirt was rumpled, his hair dishevelled and Nicola's blood heated up.

'Daddy—' Ella clasped him tight about the neck '—we have to see if Santa's been.'

Nicola shook herself, trying to dispel images that had nothing to do with Christmas and everything to do with Cade and rumpled sheets. 'We…uh…thought you might like to join us.'

'You were right.'

His blue eyes sent her a simple message—thank you. It turned her to mush.

Oh, grow a backbone, Nicola Ann!

She ousted her mother's voice from her head immediately. It was Christmas. She wasn't going to tolerate that voice today.

'Shall I lead the way?' she asked Ella.

Ella nodded and, without further ado, Nicola set off for the living room. She might not need a backbone, but a little steel in her legs wouldn't have gone amiss. The presence of warm male flesh moving so closely behind her leached the strength from her limbs with each step she took.

She hummed "Jingle Bells" under her breath in an effort to ignore and counter her traitorous body's reaction. Her newfound Christmas optimism and excitement—it left her so much more receptive to...to other things it would be wiser not to name.

She paused on the threshold of the living room, caught Ella's eye and smiled, and then with an arm partly around the little girl and partly around the father who carried her, she swept them all into the room.

Ella's eyes widened. They grew as large as frisbees as she stared at each of the stockings tacked to the mantelpiece, all full to bursting.

'See, sweetie? Didn't I tell you Santa would come?'

Ella pressed her face to Cade's neck and promptly burst into tears.

He stared at Nicola over the top of Ella's head, his eyes wide with panic.

Nicola shook her head and gave him a thumbs-up. 'Excitement,' she mouthed silently.

In no time, Ella wriggled from her father's arms and had seized her stocking, squealing in delight as she extracted her bounty.

In less than ten minutes, the rest of the family had joined them, Verity carrying Holly. With nothing to do but to watch and enjoy, Nicola sat back and took it all in, soaked up the joy and awe of the children, the warmth and affection of the adults and the promised magic of the day.

'You okay?' Cade asked, plonking himself beside her on the sofa, one of his hands resting briefly on her knee.

'Yes, of course. I...'

To her horror, she found her eyes prickling with tears. Cade's expression sharpened in a heartbeat. He moved towards her but she shook her head, gave him a thumbs-up and mouthed 'excitement' to him. He grinned then and she was grateful she witnessed it through a sheen of tears or it might well have slayed her where she sat.

When she was sure she could speak without disgracing herself, she said, 'I've never seen anything like this before except on the telly. I've never experienced this much...unadulterated joy.'

His eyes softened, those amazing blue eyes that could look as hard as the sky or as soft as a breeze, depending on their mood. 'Nic—'

'No, no.' She didn't want him feeling sorry for her. 'It's wonderful.' She beamed at him. 'I want to thank you for letting me be a part of it.'

She couldn't explain to him what a privilege she found it...or what a revelation. In Melbourne she'd developed a veneer of cynicism about Christmas to protect herself from disappointment and inevitable letdown. She realised now how self-defeating that had become. She made a vow to dispense with that cynicism for good. Christmas should never be a chore or something to run away from. It should be celebrated and cherished.

Cade tried to keep his attention on the children—on their merriment, their wide-eyed delight and their comical glee with their presents—but the smell of strawberry jam filled his senses and he found his eyes returning to Nicola again and again.

Her eyes shone with as much delight as the children's. A soft smile curved her lips. He found it particularly hard to drag his gaze from those soft, plump, kissable, strawberry-jam-scented curves. If he could have just one Christmas wish, it would be for another taste of those lips. Not a quick brush of his lips against hers, but a thorough and devastating rediscovery of their shape and texture, of their give and take, of their taste and the way her body with its killer curves melted into his when—

'Daddy?' A tug on his shirtsleeve brought him back with a start. A glance at Nicola's pink-tinged cheeks told him his hungry survey hadn't gone unobserved.

Friends! He'd promised they'd be friends. *Nothing more.*

He swiped a forearm across his brow. He had to get these darn hormones back under wraps before they flared out of control and brought him undone. But, damn it, they dodged and weaved and bucked his restraint with greater ferocity than the brumbies he'd been breaking in these last few weeks.

'Daddy?' Another tug.

'What, princess?'

'When can we open the presents under the tree?'

The presents under the tree were from the family members to each other.

Ella hopped from one foot to the other. 'I have five presents under there!'

He understood the lure and excitement of presents—he'd admit to a certain amount of curiosity about the present under there with his name on the gift tag, written in Nicola's neat schoolteacher's hand—but he didn't want his daughter growing up to think that was all Christmas was about.

'Not until after Grandma reads us the Christmas story after breakfast. Then we'll all take turns to say what we're grateful for. That was a tradition from his own childhood.

Ella leaned in close. 'I'm grapeful for lots and lots of things, Daddy.' She climbed up onto his knee and snuggled in close. 'I'm very grapeful that Santa came, that he didn't forget. And I'm grapeful that you're here and Holly and Grandma and Nic and Harry and Auntie Dee and Uncle Keith and Simon and Jamie…and that it's like a big party.' She glanced up at him. 'Aren't you grapeful for that?'

His chest expanded until he thought it might explode. He had to swallow before he could speak, infected by all that darn female emotion that had been flying around no doubt. 'You bet.'

But as Ella slid off his knee with a final squeeze, he knew he couldn't blame anyone else for the prickle of heat that threatened his eyes and his heart. He'd accomplished what he'd set out to—he'd given his daughters the Christmas they deserved. It filled him up and made him breathe easier. He would never neglect Christmas again. Never. It was too important. In a world that could be cold and brutal, it was too…necessary.

He glanced at Nicola. His children's infuriatingly delightful nanny had helped him make this day a reality, just like she'd promised she would. He wondered if she realised that was because of who she innately was, though, rather than some artificial taking part that she'd felt obliged to perform.

He closed his eyes for a moment when he recalled Ella's heartbreaking question about her mother the previous night. He was grateful now—so grateful—that Nicola had answered the way she had. There might be tears over Fran before the day was through, but Nicola was right—he could only control those things that lay in his power. Fran did not come under that particular banner. He could rest safe in the knowledge that he'd done everything he could to give his girls the Christmas they deserved. But rather than Ella or Holly, his gaze returned constantly to Nicola.

Nicola, Dee and Verity laughed in unison when they unwrapped their gifts from each other—they'd bought one another silk scarves, admired together from the same website. The children all momentarily glanced up from the *Amazing Facts* picture books and activity packs that Nicola had bought for them, but they quickly went back to oohing and ahhing over their pictures. Cade shot Harry a surreptitious glance to find she was grinning too, and sporting her Wonder Woman apron—again, one of Nicola's gifts—with pride.

He stretched his legs out, leaned back and savoured the moment. Then he seized two presents from beneath the tree and placed them into Nicola's lap.

She glanced up at him with a shy smile. 'Thank you.'

'You're welcome. Now open them.'

She tore the wrapping paper from the first, grinned and rolled her eyes. 'What are you trying to do to my waistline?' she demanded, holding up the biggest jar of chocolate-coated sultanas he'd been able to find.

'A little indulgence is good for the soul,' he countered, and then had to drag his gaze from her mouth. *That* wasn't the kind of indulgence he'd meant.

He watched as she unwrapped the second gift. Her soft 'Oh!' and wide eyes were the only thanks he needed.

'What did you get?' Dee demanded.

Nicola held up her bounty. 'Novels,' she said, and her eyes shone. 'Romance novels.'

'Ooh, that looks like a good story,' Dee said, 'and I love that author.'

'Let me see,' Verity said. 'Oh, I've read that one. It's fabulous!'

But Nicola wasn't looking at Dee or Verity, who were admiring the cache of books. She was staring straight at him with an expression that made him push his shoulders back.

'You remembered.'

'I did.' It occurred to him that, as far as Nicola went, there'd be very little he'd ever forget. Her eyes and her smile told him he'd given her the perfect present. It hadn't been much, but her true delight in the gift moved him far more than he'd expected. It made him suddenly awkward. It made him wish he could buy her a whole library of romance novels if that would make her happy.

'Open yours,' she urged with a nod towards his present under the tree. 'It's just something little. A joke really,' she said.

Her eyes danced and anticipation fizzed through him. He didn't need a second bidding. He seized the present and tore off the paper. He stared for a moment and then started to laugh. She'd given him the largest box of assorted chocolates and sweets he'd ever seen with a big *Beware* sticker plastered across the front. The accompanying note read: *Please eat in moderation!* Somehow she'd taken a bad memory, a moment of awfulness, and had turned it into something he could laugh about.

As he made a move to kiss her cheek, a second item fell out, wrapped in bubble-wrap. Intrigued, he unrolled it, and then a grin spread across his face. In his hand he held a finely wrought pewter figurine of a boxer.

Nicola grinned back at him. 'I couldn't resist.'

Verity stared from one to the other. 'I sense there's a story there.'

'Perhaps,' Nicola conceded. 'Though maybe it's more of a private joke.'

Her tact touched him, but he had no such qualms. 'Very private,' he declared, 'as I have no intention of ever telling anyone how you managed to flatten me when I gave you a boxing lesson.'

Dee promptly held her hand up and Nicola high-fived her. 'What can I say?' she said mock modestly. 'Horse-riding and boxing—it appears I'm a natural at both.'

When Dee and Verity had turned away, caught up in admiring Keith's gift to Verity—a lovely opal bracelet— Nicola nodded towards the tree again. That was when he saw a second present sporting his name on the gift tag in Nicola's handwriting. 'That one is from Ella and Holly.'

He glanced at his daughters and then ripped off the paper to find a photo frame—obviously decorated by them, no doubt with Nicola's assistance. While he instantly loved the haphazard stars and lopsided flowers painted on the frame, it was the photo that caught his attention, and held it.

Ella and Holly didn't just smile from the frame and they didn't just giggle—their entire faces and bodies glowed and roared with laughter. It spoke of their youth and their innocence, and there was no shadow of the past sixteen months there—it was a moment of straight-down-the-line exhilaration.

And it stole his breath.

He suddenly realised why this Christmas—why making it so perfect for Ella and Holly—had become so important for him. He'd been searching for optimism, for hope for the future, and an assurance that they would all be okay.

He held that assurance in his hand.

He met Nicola's gaze. 'Thank you.'

CHAPTER NINE

NICOLA paused in the doorway to the living room and drank in the stillness and silence of the Christmas night. The children had all gone to bed a couple of hours ago, and it appeared that the rest of the household had retired too.

It had been a big day.

It had been the most amazing Christmas she'd ever had.

It was getting late, but she was still too keyed up to sleep. Perhaps she just wasn't ready to let it all go yet. Sinking into the largest of the sofas, she slid sideways so she half-sat, half-lay across it, her head resting on its arm. So much fun had taken place in this room today. Her lips curved upwards as she remembered it all. And at the centre had been Cade.

Always Cade. The thought of him warmed her blood.

'I thought you'd gone to bed.'

Before she could haul herself upright again, her feet were lifted so that she lay full length on the sofa. She couldn't help groaning her appreciation at the cushioning softness that cradled her or the warmth of Cade's hands at her ankles.

With a small sliding caress, he released them and hunkered down on the floor with his back against the sofa. He smelled of soap and the single malt Scotch that he drank.

It took an effort of will not to reach out and push her fingers through his hair.

'I still feel a little too keyed up to sleep,' she admitted.

He glanced at her, the blue of his eyes a caress against her face. 'You could've settled in with one of those romance novels.'

'Ah, but then I'd be up all night devouring it.'

He opened his mouth, but then his eyes stilled, his gaze seemingly arrested by her lips—arrested and absorbed. It made her blood chug and it chased her tiredness away in the time it took the lights on the Christmas tree to wink on and then off. And the longer he stared, the more she remembered the feel of his lips on hers and the taste of him, and the yearning, the craving, built inside her until she had to cover her mouth with her hand to stop him from looking at her like that.

He jolted away from her, his gaze shooting to the Christmas tree. She closed her eyes and tried to get her breathing back under control. 'I...' She swallowed. 'It's been a great day. You must be over the moon. You gave Ella a Christmas she'll remember for ever, and Holly had a ball. Not to mention the rest of your family.'

'And you?'

When he turned back it was almost as if that earlier moment hadn't happened. Her heart burned in protest even as her common sense told her it was for the best. 'I've had the best Christmas ever.' Her voice emerged on a husky whisper. She couldn't help it. 'What about you? Did you enjoy today or were you too preoccupied with making sure everyone else had a good time?'

He lifted his tumbler, breathed in the fumes, but he didn't drink. 'I had a great day.' He started to lift the tumbler to his lips and then paused and offered her the glass.

She wrinkled her nose and shook her head. 'I'm not a

fan of whisky.' Not even the gorgeous single malt Scotch that had been Verity's gift to Cade. 'I prefer something sweeter.'

He took a sip and his eyes suddenly gleamed. 'Something sweeter, huh?'

'I'm fine, Cade. I don't want anything, honestly.'

'I noticed you didn't stuff yourself senseless at lunch like the rest of us and then spend the afternoon nibbling on all the assorted goodies.'

'I ate my fair share, thank you very much!' She just hadn't gone back for seconds. And she hadn't picked too much between meals—other than a couple of handfuls of cherries. She was still intent on slimming down.

She had slimmed down.

Today had shown her just how much she'd always comfort ate at Christmas…and how much she comfort ate full stop. She didn't want to do that any more.

'Yet you have a sweet tooth.'

'That I'm doing my best to control.' She wasn't given to pats on the back—not for herself—but she couldn't help feeling she deserved a big fat pat on the back for that. There had been moments when that self-control had been sheer torture.

'You have a sweet tooth,' he repeated, 'and it's Christmas.'

She didn't trust that gleam in his eye. 'So?'

He slid across the floor and seized her jar of chocolate sultanas and lifted them in her direction. Her mouth promptly watered. No amount of self-control could prevent that.

She tried to distract herself. 'Harry and your mother wouldn't let me tidy up.' Presents still sat in festive stacks about the room.

'Absolutely not. That's what Boxing Day is for.'

He said it exactly the same way Verity had.

He shook the jar. 'Nicola, these are unopened.'

The sound of chocolate sultanas tinkling against glass sounded like raindrops hitting parched earth and cued more mouth watering. 'I…um…' She stared at the jar. Simon had kindly informed her that its contents looked like kangaroo droppings, but not even that thought could stop her from salivating. She swallowed. 'I'm saving them for when there's not quite so many other nibblies around.'

'You're not bringing these out to share with anyone.'

She wasn't?

'They are all yours.'

Her heart thudded in anticipation…and greed.

He slid back over to the sofa, bringing the jar with him. He broke the seal. 'Oops.'

His utter lack of remorse should've made her laugh, only he waved the jar under her nose and the combined scent of chocolate and sultana hit her. Her stomach clenched. Her resolve faltered.

'They're open now.'

The invitation in his voice could tempt a stronger woman than her. She forced herself to think of Melbourne, of Diane and Brad…and her mother. She sat up. She planted her feet on the floor. 'Then by all means help yourself to as many as you'd like.'

The gleam didn't leave his eyes, but a new determination entered them as he planted himself on the sofa beside her. He tipped a pile of the confectionery into his hand and held it out towards her. Taking one sultana, he lifted it to his lips and ate it slowly. 'Mmm…delicious.'

For a moment she couldn't move. She wanted to yell at him for tempting her resolve so outrageously.

A second sultana followed suit. That hand waved temptingly beneath her nose.

He lifted a third…

She could stand it no longer. She seized a sultana from his cupped hand and popped it straight into her mouth. The chocolate melted on her tongue. When she bit down, the flavour of the sultana exploded through her. She groaned and closed her eyes in ecstasy.

When he took her hand and poured the sultanas into them, she made no protest. She ate them, savoured them.

He watched her devour them. The gleam had left his eyes, replaced with something she couldn't read and was too cowardly to decipher.

'You really do love them.' His voice was low.

'They're my favourite food on earth.'

'Then why deny yourself? Especially today?'

The pile he'd tipped into her hand had gone. She'd eaten them all. And she wanted more. Lots more.

Are you going to be a complete glutton, Nicola Ann?

With a gulp, she seized the lid and tried to put it back on the jar, only Cade wouldn't let her. He captured her hand, his grip tightening until she looked at him. 'Why deny yourself?'

Her pulse throbbed at the contact. She tried to shrug. 'Once I start eating them, I can't stop.'

'And what's wrong with that?'

He couldn't be serious? 'If I keep eating them, I will get fat. Fatter,' she amended. 'How on earth will I lose weight if I keep indulging?'

'So you won't even allow yourself the occasional in-dulgence?'

'It's dangerous to indulge a weakness.'

His eyes narrowed. He poured more sultanas into his hand and held one out to her. She swallowed. She tried to say no, but his eyes urged her to throw caution to the winds, to live in the moment.

She opened her mouth, helpless to resist either Cade

or the sweet, and savoured every delicious moment of the morsel.

'It's ludicrous to deny yourself such a simple pleasure.'

It wasn't simple, though. She couldn't help but feel this lack of self-control was somehow tied into being treated so badly by Diane and Brad...and all her friends thinking her a doormat. Slimming down, brightening herself up and not allowing herself to be taken for granted would prove to them all that she wasn't a doormat. Or a failure.

He held another sultana up, she opened her mouth and he slipped it between her lips. The inherent sensuality of the gesture was as delicious as the chocolate and sultana combination. 'Would you be happier if you were thin?'

She blinked. 'Well, hello, yes!' Any woman would say yes to that.

He slammed the jar of sultanas onto the coffee table. 'Why the hell is that so? What the hell is wrong with your body? I *love* your body. I can't stand that you hate it.' He ground his teeth together and then poured more sultanas into her hand. 'Your worth is not measured by your weight or your waistline. Eat!'

He loved her body? With tears prickling the backs of her eyes, she ate.

Finally she had to lean back with a groan and shake her head. 'If I have any more I'll be ill.'

Only then did Cade replace the lid on the jar. He turned back to her. 'What do you think losing weight will prove to Diane and Brad...or your mother?'

His perception froze her.

'That you have worth?'

If she said yes, would he yell at her again?

'It's not your weight that's the problem, Nicola, it's your attitude. Until you learn to embrace your body, to love it as you should love it because it's beautiful, then nobody else is going to give you the respect you deserve.'

He reached out and cupped her cheek. His hand smelled of chocolate. She wanted to close her eyes and breathe him in. 'We teach people how to treat us. You don't need to lose weight. You need to learn to walk tall—with pride and confidence.'

She thought about that, and about the way Verity and Dee carried themselves. The way Cade carried himself. They walked with pride and confidence, as if they were sure of who they were and their place in the world.

Growing up with her mother's constant stream of criticism had eroded her confidence and sense of self-worth, but she wasn't a child any longer. She was an adult, able to make her own value judgements, and there were a lot of things she could do well. She was a good teacher and a good friend. She could ride a horse as if it were second nature. When she sang, people stopped to listen. She believed in the values of compassion, kindness and justice.

'Well?'

She stared into his eyes and realised she couldn't believe those values held true for other people and not for herself too. Values didn't work that way.

She blinked, stunned by the revelation. 'I think,' she started slowly, 'that you might be right. I mean, it's such a simple truth but…' She'd never seen it before.

Finally he smiled and it was like Christmas all over again. She leaned forward and kissed his cheek. 'Thank you.'

He stilled. His gaze lowered to her lips and his eyes darkened. Heat threaded through her…and temptation.

'You should go to bed.'

The words growled out of him, but his gaze remained on her lips, the hunger in them identical to her hunger for the chocolate sultanas. It was then she realised there was something she craved more than those—Cade. She wanted him with an elemental savagery that shook her bones.

She should move away and go to bed like he'd ordered, but Cade had set something free in her tonight when he'd tempted her with those sultanas and told her he loved her body. He'd made her face temptation head-on. He'd forced her to indulge it. Now she had no hope of resisting the greater temptation he presented. She had no desire to do so.

She slipped her hands either side of his face and, leaning forward, placed her lips on his. She tasted of chocolate, he tasted of whisky, and the combination of flavours was as heady as anything she had ever experienced.

He held himself still beneath her touch, but he didn't pull away and, emboldened, she moved in closer to deepen the kiss and taste him more fully.

A breath shuddered out of him. Her hands explored the angle of his jaw, the strong line of his neck and shoulders. One of her hands snaked around his head to anchor her more firmly against him while her other splayed across his chest, revelling in the male strength of him.

With that movement it was as if she had released some check or restraint in him. With a groan, he gathered her close and claimed her lips with a potent mastery that had her trembling and reeling both at the same time.

His hand moved to the hem of her shirt, and then under it. The skin on skin contact made her gasp as a delicious new energy and a brand new greed fired through her. He pressed her back against the sofa, angling her beneath him as his lips and tongue teased her lips and tongue, and all she could do was cling to him. One powerful thigh insinuated its way between her legs. She arched against it, wanting to feel him pressed against all of her, gripped by a need bigger than herself.

He'd fed her chocolate sultanas. He'd told her he loved her body. He kissed her exactly how she'd always needed to be kissed but had never been kissed before. The man was perfect!

With a growl, she reached up and tore the buttons from his shirt, raked her fingernails down his bare chest. He hissed in a breath and she revelled in the freedom of touching him. She pressed her palms to his hot skin and breathed him in. He was hard and as smooth as satin.

Perfect!

Slowly, deliciously, she moved her hands down to his stomach. He trembled. Had she done that? She did it again. He trembled again and she revelled in the knowledge that she could affect all of this superb masculinity so easily, with just a touch.

Beneath her shirt, his hand moved to cover one breast. Beneath the thin cotton of her bra her nipple puckered and tautened. He rolled it between thumb and forefinger.

'Oh!' She stiffened and then arched into his touch, her body jerking in reaction, and that slow, lazy smile that she loved so much spread across his face as he continued to torment her fevered flesh.

Boldly, she ran her fingers beneath the waistband of his jeans and the laziness vanished. 'Kiss me,' she groaned. It was half an order and half a plea. He complied and Nicola lost herself in a world of sensation.

Completely. Time held no sway. There was only Cade and her…and magic.

'Daddy?'

A foreign sound filtered into her consciousness and Nicola stilled.

'Nic?'

Cade froze.

It hit her then what the interruption was—Ella!

She and Cade sprang apart. Nicola righted her clothes and pasted on a bright smile for Ella's benefit. 'Hey, pumpkin.'

She glanced at Cade, expecting him to look as discomposed as she felt. He didn't. He'd gone cold and still. He'd withdrawn, utterly and completely. Her stomach dropped and her skin chilled. He'd thrown up a brick wall, complete with razor wire and a watchtower. His body gave off wave after wave of rebuttal and rejection. She wanted to close her eyes so she didn't have to witness it. She wanted to shake him. She wanted...

It didn't matter what she wanted.

'What's up, sweetie?' Her voice came out surprisingly steady, although her insides trembled and her knees felt like jelly. 'What are you doing up?'

Ella raced across to bury her face in Nicola's lap. 'I'm thirsty. I want a drink of water.'

'Oh, I think we can manage that.' She brushed a hand through the child's hair.

She kept her voice deliberately cheerful, even while inside she was dying. Dying of embarrassment and something darker and harder and meaner, although she couldn't put a name to it. But it reared up to stab her every time she glanced at the hard, uncompromising line of Cade's mouth.

'I'll take care of this.'

With an effortless ease that spoke of his strength—and resolve—he lifted Ella into his arms.

'Go to bed, Nicola.'

He turned and walked away. And just like that she was dismissed.

She sat there, stunned, unable to move as her body attempted to process the emotions that tumbled through her in a confusing jumbled rush—the memory of Cade's mouth on hers, with its searing heat, the way her body had come alive in his arms, the way she'd forgotten herself completely…and then the chilled recognition of his withdrawal.

Her hands clenched. She should feel grateful for the interruption, but all she felt was a frustrated sense of disappointment, and it grew and prickled and itched. She would get no sleep tonight.

She rose, Cade's curt and dismissive *Go to bed, Nicola* still ringing in her ears, when a sudden chill dissipated all of her built up heat.

Her arms snaked about her waist. Her mouth dried. What on earth had she been thinking? If they hadn't been interrupted, she and Cade would've gone all the way. They'd have made love. And then what?

She wrung her hands and then gripped them tightly. What was wrong with her? Did she mean to transfer all the dreams she'd had for the future—marriage, babies and a home—to the first man she met? Was she really that weak and needy?

Her chin snapped up. While she suspected Cade wasn't in the right head space to contemplate that kind of commitment, she knew for sure that she wasn't. Her life was complicated enough as it was. She wasn't going to make it even more complicated.

Go to bed, Nicola.

She went to bed.

'What's your New Year resolution, Nicola, darling?'

Nicola started when Verity directed the question at her. It shouldn't have; almost everyone else in the room had taken a turn. Verity wanted to learn Irish dancing. Keith wanted to complete a marathon. Dee wanted to lose weight, which had made everyone laugh with its predictability and droll delivery.

Nicola planned to incorporate a lot of changes into her life when she returned to Melbourne, but what would she choose as her New Year resolution? It had to be something special.

'You don't have to tell us if it's too personal, darling.'

'Oh, it's not that. It's just...' She pushed her shoulders back. 'This year I want to make my resolution matter, and I want to keep it.'

She could feel Cade's eyes on her—their penetrating heat and intelligence. She refused to turn and meet his gaze, afraid of what her face might reveal. They'd carefully skirted around each other this week, kept their dealings short and professional, had never once mentioned their out of control Christmas kiss, but she suspected one look would reveal the desire she tried to keep in check. If an answering desire flared in his eyes she'd be lost. And she didn't want to be lost.

'Okay.' She straightened in her easy chair—she and Cade didn't share a sofa any more. 'This year I will not avoid confrontation if keeping the peace is at my own expense. This last year has shown me that keeping the peace for everyone else's sake is not always good for me.'

'Wow,' Dee breathed. 'That's a tough one.'

Nicola wrinkled her nose. 'Especially as I hate confrontation.'

'You've made me feel shallow.'

'Oh, and I forgot to add that I want to lose five kilos too.'

As she hoped, everyone laughed.

'Cade, darling, what's your resolution?'

She could still feel his gaze on her. She schooled her face and turned her head to meet it.

'Nicola has taught me something this last month.'

She had? He smiled and it was so unexpected she had to smile back. Everyone leaned forward, eager to hear what he had to say.

'I directed all my energies into making Christmas wonderful for the girls—for everyone else too, but primarily for the girls.'

They all nodded.

'I realise now I should be directing my energies into making the rest of the year just as good.'

The breath whooshed out of her. She'd taught him that?

'It's time to look to the future instead of the past. That's what I'll be working on this year.'

'Amen,' Verity said softly. 'Ooh, look, it's nearly time for the countdown to midnight. Keith and Cade, top up everyone's glasses while I turn on the radio.'

They all stood and counted down the final ten seconds to midnight and the brand new year. Nicola prayed that this year she would be able to hold her head high and prove her worth—to herself. It had become less and less important to prove it to anyone else.

'Happy New Year!' all of Cade's family called out, clinking champagne flutes. Then there were hugs and kisses.

'Happy New Year, Nicola.' Cade kissed her cheek and then backed off in super-quick time.

'Happy New Year,' she said, fighting a sense of awkwardness. 'Nice resolution, boss man.'

'Right back at you,' he returned.

He grinned. She smiled. And the awkwardness slipped away and it felt as if their friendship was back on track. And it felt right…even if she had to tamp down on the desire that threaded through her.

'Okay, bedtime for me,' Verity declared. 'Especially if I'm to wake in time for the traditional New Year trek.'

Nicola glanced at Verity. 'Traditional trek?'

They all turned to stare at her. 'Hasn't anybody mentioned Lake Campbell to you, darling?'

Umm…no.

At her blank look, Cade said, 'Every New Year's Day we pack a picnic and head out to the lake. It's a bit of a trek as the lake is two hours away, but…'

'But the children love it,' Dee said, picking up where Cade left off. 'The swimming and the change of scenery.'

'So do the adults.' Verity smiled. 'I know you're used to the coast and the seaside, but the lake is a lovely place to swim, and it's a beautiful spot. I promise you'll enjoy it.'

'I don't doubt that for a moment. It sounds lovely,' Nicola said. It would be wonderful to experience more of this compelling Outback landscape. 'You'll have to excuse me from the swimming, though. I'm afraid I didn't bring a swimming costume.' She hadn't expected to need one.

'The kids won't let you get away with that,' Dee said. 'You've become too firm a favourite. Besides, we play lots of water games and it would be a shame to sit those out. I'll lend you a cossie. We're about the same size.' She suddenly chuckled. 'After all, I did bring four with me.'

Keith shook his head. 'The woman has no concept of packing light.'

Dee slapped him playfully and then her eyes gleamed in a way that reminded Nicola of Cade. 'In fact, I know the exact costume that would suit you best.'

All through this exchange she was aware of Cade's watchful surveillance. The thought of appearing in front of him in a swimsuit… Something inside her trembled. She forced a smile. 'Lovely, thank you.'

As they all drifted away to their separate bedrooms to

retire for the night, it occurred to her that tomorrow Cade would appear before her in nothing but a swimsuit as well.

She couldn't quite stamp out the anticipation that threaded through her.

'What do you think?' Cade asked as she climbed from the ute.

For a moment Nicola couldn't form a coherent sentence. The wild beauty of Cade's lake stole her breath. Never in her wildest dreams had she ever imagined that such a place could exist, or that she'd ever be lucky enough to visit it.

They'd arrived along a long, low, green-brown plain that had extended for mile upon mile and had lulled her with its unending monotony, but that was all at her back. In front of her stretched a large lake, bordered on its far side by a wall of orange and yellow rock that curved at least halfway around towards them. Not even a breeze ruffled the calm surface of the water that reflected back the sky's perfect blue. Paper daisies dotted the shore and a flock of pink cockatoos squalled in a stand of tall skinny gum trees off to her left. 'It's an oasis,' she breathed.

Holly's imperious squeal from her child's seat in the back of the car had her swinging away from the amazing view. 'I'll get her,' Cade said, grinning at whatever he saw in her face.

Ella slipped her hand into Nicola's. 'This is one of my favourite places ever.'

'Mine too,' Nicola found herself agreeing.

It was an almost perfect day. Everyone was in a determined holiday mood and, as Verity explained to her, this really was the last hurrah for their holiday. Tomorrow, she, Dee, Keith and the twins would be returning to Brisbane and 'the real world' as she called it.

The borrowed swimsuit wasn't an exercise in self-conscious agony either. For a start, it wasn't the bikini she'd feared but a one-piece that nipped her in nicely at the waist, even if the bust line plunged much lower than she was used to.

The expression on Cade's face when he first saw her in it made that more than worthwhile. It made her feel beautiful, glamorous even. And then she'd taken in his bare chest and shoulders—the latent power and strength of him on display—and heat had shimmered between them with a dangerous intensity that had held them both in thrall.

Someone's laughter had broken the spell. Cade had turned and plunged into the lake and Nicola had been able to breathe again. After that they were careful to avoid eye contact.

They all swam. They joked and laughed. They played water cricket. They relaxed on the shore and demolished the picnic Harry had packed for them. When offered, Nicola took two whole handfuls of chocolate sultanas and savoured every single one of them. They dozed under makeshift shelters during the worst of the heat and then swam again.

And all the while Nicola was aware of Cade's compelling presence. Of his ease and patience with the children. Of his courtesy to his mother and sister...and to her. And of the undisputed beauty of his body.

In the evening the men built a contained campfire. Not for warmth but to toast marshmallows. It was the perfect end to the perfect day.

Ella planted herself on Nicola's lap, her head resting in the hollow of Nicola's shoulder. Her clean wholesome smell, her soft weight, stirred all of Nicola's not so latent maternal instincts and created an ache deep inside.

She did her best to ignore it. One day maybe she'd be

lucky enough to have a little girl as loving and trusting as Ella. She pulled Ella close for a hug and to plant a kiss on the crown of her head.

'I had the best day in the world, Nic.'

'Me too, sweetie.'

The child was silent for a while and Nicola thought she'd fallen asleep. 'I wish you were my mummy.'

Ella's words were clear in the evening air and rang out around the circle they'd formed about the campfire. Nicola didn't dare look at any of the other adults. Not that she would've seen them for the sudden tears that blinded her. She blinked hard, but nothing could clear the ache that stretched her throat…or the bigger one settling in her chest.

'Honey…' she swallowed '…I think that's just about the nicest thing anyone has ever said to me.'

Ella suddenly straightened. 'Daddy, you could marry Nic. I know you like her because I saw you kissing her.'

CHAPTER TEN

ELLA'S innocently revealing words punched the air from Cade's lungs, robbing him of the ability to speak. It was all he could do to stay upright and not fall face first in the dirt.

To his infinite relief, his mother and Dee tactfully started to pack things away in preparation for the return journey. They didn't raise enquiring or teasing eyebrows in his direction or shoot him sidelong glances. He loved them for the space they gave him, the way they respected his privacy. He'd neglected them this last year and they'd borne it without complaint. He would never be able to thank them enough for their patience.

It didn't mean he could move to help them clean up now, though. It didn't mean he could think of anything to say to ease the situation.

I wish you were my mummy. The words froze him all over again. His temples throbbed. His eyes ached. All he could do was stare at Nicola and pray that...

What? That she could make this right?

I wish you were my mummy. He swallowed the bile that burned acid in his throat.

He had no idea how Nicola managed to maintain her composure, but she did, and while it was true that colour heightened her cheeks, she didn't stumble as she explained to Ella that the kiss the child had witnessed had only been a friendly kiss and that she and Daddy were just good friends. She didn't laugh at Ella, which would've cut the child to the quick. He was seized with a sudden fierce desire to hug her for her easy, confident manner with his daughter. With both his daughters.

'But I don't want you to leave Waminda!' Ella suddenly wailed.

A chill trickled down his spine. He should've seen this coming—the fact that Ella might form an attachment to her temporary nanny. He should've taken it into account, but he'd been too hell-bent on ensuring Christmas went off without a hitch to have considered the possibility.

Perspiration prickled his scalp, his nape, his top lip. After Fran's desertion, it was a possibility he should've considered. He'd left Ella open for rejection, not just by one woman, but by two. His hands clenched. His jaw clenched. He wanted to throw his head back and howl at the mess he'd made of things.

'I love it at Waminda too.' Nicola's voice sounded clear and harmonious in the evening air. It filtered through the furore raging in his mind and somehow helped to soothe it, though he didn't know how.

'But you always knew I had to go back to my home in Melbourne. I have to go back to see my mother and my friends…and I have to go back to my job, remember?'

'As a schoolteacher.' Ella nodded, evidently proud that she'd remembered.

'But it doesn't mean we can't be best friends for ever, though, does it? We can write to each other—letters and emails. That'll be fun, don't you think?'

Ella nodded again. And then she straightened and started to bounce. 'We could Skype!'

His four-year-old had recently discovered the joys of the Internet and particularly Skype. His lips twisted. He could forsee a Skype addiction in the future. But suddenly that didn't seem so bad, because Ella wasn't crying or traumatised by the thought of Nicola's departure from Waminda.

Nicola had managed to quieten Ella's fears and at the same time pump up the little girl's confidence with an ease he couldn't believe. It occurred to him then that she might have foreseen a moment like this, and had come up with a plan that she'd implemented so smoothly nobody's feelings were hurt and all seemed right with the world. Only...

In another three weeks, Nicola *would* leave Waminda, and that suddenly seemed very, very wrong.

He shot to his feet and immediately set about helping with the general clearing up and packing away. They always made an effort to leave the lake and surrounding as untouched as they could.

I wish you were my mummy.

The words burned like a brand. His gaze drifted to Ella and Nicola and his heart clenched at the way Ella rested against Nicola with all the trust in her four-year-old heart. And at the way Nicola held the child as if she were the most precious thing in the world.

Ella deserved a mother—a woman who would love her and provide her with a role model.

Nicola deserved the family, the children her heart craved.

Daddy, you could marry Nic.

The insidious thought slid under his guard and chafed at him. He tried to shake it off. It was a crazy idea.

I saw you kissing her.

His mouth dried. There was no doubt whatsoever that he enjoyed kissing her. No doubt whatsoever that he'd like to do a whole lot more than kiss her.

But marry her?

He shook his head with a muttered curse and set about packing the car.

Cade, Nicola, Ella and Holly—with a little help from Nicola—waved at the plane as it took off into endless and cloudless blue sky.

Ella slipped her hand inside Cade's. 'I'll miss Grandma, Daddy.'

'Me too.' It took him a moment to drag his gaze from the way Nicola kissed Holly's crown and then made her giggle by tickling her. He forced himself to smile down at Ella. 'But she'll visit again soon,' he assured her, ushering them back to the car and helping Ella with her seat belt while Nicola strapped Holly into her car seat.

'She said she'd visit for my birthday.'

He nodded as he started the car and turned it in the direction of the homestead. Dee was going to do her best to bring the boys back for a couple of days then too. He hoped he'd be able to return the favour and take Ella and Holly to visit for the twins' birthdays later in the year.

'Nic, can you come back for my birthday?'

Nicola stiffened. If he hadn't been so finely attuned to her every movement he'd have missed it, it was so fleeting. But he was attuned. And he didn't miss it.

He glanced at her sharply, but she barely met his gaze as she turned to talk to Ella in the back seat. 'When's your birthday, sweetie?'

'Um…Daddy?'

'The eleventh of March.'

Nicola shook her head. 'That's in term time so I won't be able to make it.'

In the rear-vision mirror he watched the joy leach from Ella's face.

'But it doesn't mean I can't come to visit in holiday time...or that I can't send you a present,' she added on a teasing note.

Both assurances made Ella brighten, but they didn't satisfy him. 'What about Easter?' he found himself demanding. 'Could you come then?'

She met his gaze but he couldn't read her expression and he had to drag his attention back to the dusty track before he drove over a mulga bush or fallen log or large rock and ripped a hole in the fuel tank or tore the muffler from the car.

'I'm afraid not.'

'You have plans?' He couldn't let it go.

'I do.'

There was nothing left to say after that.

Something dragged Cade from the depths of sleep. He sat up in bed and tried to shake the fog from his brain so he could identify what had woken him.

Crying... Holly...

He was on his feet in an instant and stumbling in the direction of the nursery.

He paused in the doorway. Nicola was already there. She had Holly in her arms and was walking her up and down singing a low lullaby. He noticed the bottle of baby medicine on the nightstand.

When she turned to walk back towards the doorway and saw him, she shot him a smile that reassured him there was nothing seriously wrong with his youngest daughter. In time and tune to her lullaby, she sang, 'We're teething, Daddy, and it's not very comfortable.'

Holly's cries were starting to ease. Poor little tyke. He wanted to reach out and cradle her head, only he didn't want to disturb her now she was starting to settle again.

Nicola sang that he should go back to bed.

He should. He needed to be up early in the morning—as usual—but he found he didn't want to. He found the sight of Nicola in her nightie, rocking his child to sleep, amazingly comforting…and undeniably erotic. It struck him as unbelievably tantalising when he realised how thin her nightdress was, and how he could almost make out her entire shape beneath it.

His nanny was all woman and pure temptation. When she leant over the cot his breath caught at the free sway of her breasts. He could imagine the weight of them in his hands, he could imagine burying his face in them and the way she would arch against him and—

'Cade, go to bed. Holly is sleeping now. I'm sorry we woke you.'

She'd settled Holly with a minimum of fuss. She was great with her. She was great with both his daughters.

'Can we talk?' The question shot out of him before he realised he'd meant to ask it. But after a moment's thought he didn't regret it. Not one little bit. He pushed his shoulders back.

'Cade, it's one o'clock in the morning.'

'But—'

'This is not a good time for us to talk.' She swallowed. 'It's not a good time for us to be alone.'

When she went to ease past him, he used his body to trap her against the doorframe. His chest touched her chest and he could feel the way her breath caught and her nipples peaked. His groin hardened in instant response. He prayed she'd stay.

With a shuddering breath, she pushed him away. 'In the morning, Cade. We'll talk then,' she choked out, and then she fled down the hallway to her own room.

His hand curled to a fist. He rested his forehead against

the doorframe and bit back a curse. That hadn't been the smartest move he'd ever made. He'd promised he would just be a good friend, but...

But the moment he saw her all good intentions flew out of his head. He'd better get his damn hormones back under control by morning, though, because he and Nicola were going to have a talk. And he meant to keep it completely professional.

He pushed away from the door and headed for his en suite bathroom. He needed a cold shower.

Breakfast the next morning was hell. Every time Nicola's mouth closed about her toast or touched the rim of her mug, his body reacted with the memory of those lips on his flesh and the fire they could send shooting through his veins.

When she reached for the strawberry jam, he shot to his feet. 'When you're done here, could you come to my study?'

She blinked at his abruptness. 'Yes, of course.'

Professional, level-headed, he schooled himself as he strode away. He wanted Nicola to stay at Waminda Downs permanently and he had to outline to her in as attractive a way as possible all the reasons why that was a good idea. Hormones would not help him there.

Less than ten minutes later she appeared in his study doorway. He motioned for her to take the seat across the desk from him. He did his best not to notice the soft plumpness of her lips and to close his mind to the scent of strawberry jam. It wasn't easy, especially as some time during the last few weeks she'd started wearing clothes that accentuated her stunning figure rather than hide it, clothes that highlighted the colour of her hair and eyes and made her skin glow. He gritted his teeth.

'You wanted to talk to me?' she prompted.

He kicked himself into gear. 'Nicola, I want you to consider taking on the role of Ella and Holly's nanny full-time. Both of them adore you and you've fitted in so well at Waminda Downs. Having you here has made me realise that we do, in fact, need a full-time nanny.'

It wasn't fair to ask Harry to take on so much of the child-minding duties on top of all her other chores. Having Nicola here had freed up both him and Harry. He couldn't deny he'd enjoyed the opportunity to work around the station more these last few weeks—had rediscovered his love for a good day's work.

'I believe you're right and you do need a full-time nanny, but, Cade, although I'm touched you asked me first, the answer is no.'

His head snapped back. For a moment he couldn't speak. 'But…but you haven't even taken the time to consider it yet.' His mouth opened and closed. He fought a scowl. 'I thought you liked it here. I thought you loved Holly and Ella.'

'I adore them!' She leaned forward. 'And I have enjoyed it here, but I made it clear from the first that this was a time-out for me and not a permanent venture.'

His hands clenched. 'Why can't you reconsider all that now—?'

'I love my job as a schoolteacher.' She sat back. 'I've worked hard to get where I am. Becoming a nanny would not be making the best use of my skills. It would, in fact, be a demotion.'

'I can afford to pay you your current salary.' Plus more.

'It's not about the money, Cade!' Her eyes suddenly spat fire. 'Look, I have no intention of burying myself out here as if I'm afraid to return home, as if I can't hold my head up and meet anyone's eyes square-on.'

She wouldn't even take a few days to think about his

offer? He slashed a hand through the air. She was perfect for his daughters. And they were perfect for her. If only she'd see it. 'That's just misplaced pride!'

'No, it's not.' Her eyes didn't flash fire any more. She looked cool. Too cool. 'Besides, it's sensible. Down the track, I want to marry and have children of my own. Who am I going to meet out here?'

The thought of another man kissing those luscious lips fired him with an anger he knew he had no right to feel. An unreasonable, unholy anger. He bit back the torrent that clawed at his throat. Think. *Think!* It would be in everyone's best interests if she stayed.

She wanted to be a mother.

He wanted a mother for his children.

He shot to his feet. 'Then marry me, Nicola. That way we can both have what we want.'

Nicola recoiled from Cade and his outrageous suggestion.

He strode around the desk. She shot to her feet but he caught her hand before she could back away.

'Think about it,' he urged in that silky voice that could tempt a saint.

She had thought about it! The life here—her soul craved it. It seemed perfect.

Except...

He didn't love her. And she wasn't sure if she loved him. Lust wasn't love. Nor was a desire for a family. She would not be weak and stupid, as she had been with Brad. She meant to be very sure of her reasons the next time she decided to marry.

If there is a next time, Nicola Ann. At your age there certainly aren't any guarantees.

She swallowed.

'I have a family that would embrace and welcome you.

We'd have more children, of course. We could have as many as you wanted.'

How many more offers of marriage do you expect to receive?

'And you can't deny there's heat between us. It would be very pleasurable creating those babies.'

She couldn't deny that. And she couldn't deny the empty ache that filled her whenever she thought of having children of her own and wondering if that would ever happen, but…

He lifted her chin to meet his gaze, his fingers caressing the skin there. 'I would be faithful to you. I would do whatever I could to make you happy.'

He meant every word; she could see that. She swallowed the lump in her throat. 'You don't love me.'

'I like you. I enjoy spending time with you. I desire you. And you love my daughters. What more could I possibly need?'

'Love.'

He frowned. 'You said the next time you decided to marry, you'd make sure you got exactly what you wanted from the relationship.' He eased back, his eyes serious. 'I am offering you exactly what you want.'

She had to bite her tongue. She had to swallow and then draw in a deep breath. No matter how much this man with his angry wounded eyes and his lips that could transport her to heaven tempted her, she would not make the same mistake she had in the past. 'I was wrong and misguided when I said those things. I was feeling hurt and angry and I wanted to lash out. I wanted to find a way to protect myself, but it was all a lie.'

She pulled herself up to her full height. 'Since I've been here I've come to see how wrong that kind of thinking is. If I treated someone that callously and with that degree of calculation it would make me worse than Brad and Diane. I have no intention of…of being such a bitch.'

His eyes narrowed. 'Love is an overrated emotion and—'

'And it's precisely what I need, and I won't settle for anything less.' She snatched her hand from his. 'I need love *and* friendship.' Her eyes burned and her throat thickened. 'You made me believe in friendship again, but it was a lie. You don't care what's best for me. All you care about is what's best for your daughters and you're more than willing to sacrifice me on that particular altar, aren't you?'

'I—'

'But if you think a loveless marriage is what's best for Ella and Holly then you are truly and utterly mistaken.' She heaved in a breath, taken off guard by the pain that sliced through her. 'There are a lot of nannies out there who would bond with Ella and Holly as well as I have done and whom you wouldn't have to make the supreme sacrifice of marrying.'

He clenched his jaw so hard white lines appeared around his mouth. 'I wouldn't consider marrying you a sacrifice,' he ground out.

For a moment she almost believed him. She gave a harsh laugh and shook her head. 'You are so not ready to get remarried. Are you telling me you're prepared to give another woman the chance to walk out on you and the girls again? Because what makes you so sure I wouldn't, huh?'

His head snapped back. 'I know you. I know you wouldn't do that.'

Really? She folded her arms. 'Let's just play with another scenario for a moment. What if I said I would marry you and Fran heard about it and, as a result, came racing back here to ask you for a second chance? After all, she is

Ella and Holly's mother. Who would you choose? Which of us would you deem as the best choice for your daughters?'

His face, his frame, his fists all tightened. 'That is not going to happen!'

'That's not an answer, Cade.' A terrible tiredness gripped her. Her temples throbbed and her hands shook. Perspiration prickled her nape. 'And until you do know the answer you're in no fit state to marry anyone.'

She recognised the panic that raced across his face then too but she had to harden her heart against it before it led her into doing something she'd regret.

She folded her arms. 'Marrying you would not be the best thing for me.'

Beneath his tan, he paled.

You stupid girl, Nicola Ann!

She lifted her chin. 'I deserve better.'

She turned and left the room. He didn't try to stop her.

The next fifteen days were a new kind of hell, one Nicola had never experienced before. Cade barely spoke to her and yet as each day passed she could hardly bear the thought of leaving Waminda Downs—of leaving Jack and Scarlett and Harry; of leaving Ella and Holly.

Of leaving Cade.

Her heart lurched and ached with each reminder of the hours that passed and the diminishing time that was left to her here. Somehow this place and these people had soaked into her bones.

She hadn't fallen in love with Cade, though. She refused to believe that.

Leaving day finally arrived, and the moment the Cessna left the ground to wing her away on the first leg of her journey home to Melbourne, Nicola burst into tears.

'Sorry,' she mumbled to the pilot—Jerry, who'd brought

her to Waminda Downs seven weeks ago—as he handed her a handkerchief. 'It's just I'm going to miss them all so much.'

He nodded. 'Those little girls are the sweetest things. Kids, huh? They wrap themselves around your heart.'

They were...and they had. But it was Cade's face that rose in her mind. With each mile that took her further away, the more it felt as if her heart was being ripped from her chest.

CHAPTER ELEVEN

Four months later...

NICOLA slipped the orange chiffon dress over her head and smoothed it down across her hips as her mother tied the halter neck into a bow at Nicola's nape, and then adjusted the plunging neckline for a flattering and dramatic effect.

'Nicola Ann, you look lovely. You'll outshine the bride herself.' Angela McGillroy's lips pressed together. 'Not that she doesn't deserve it.'

Nicola suppressed a smile. Her mother's attitude had undergone an amazing transformation ever since a particularly frank and terse discussion they'd had when Nicola had returned from Waminda Downs. She had unequivocally told her mother that if she wanted to maintain a relationship with her, the constant stream of criticism and nit-picking had to stop. She'd told her that the way she chose to live her life was her affair—if it made her happy, why did her mother have such a problem with it?

Her mother hadn't been able to speak for a full thirty seconds. 'But Nicola Ann,' she'd finally said, 'all I want is for you to be happy. I just never thought you were.'

'Maybe because I never am when I'm around you. You always make me feel I'm a disappointment, that I never measure up.'

'Oh, Nicola, why have you never told me this before? I've been pushing the things that make me happy in the hope that they'd help. They weren't supposed to make you unhappier! It's just...that's the way I was raised.'

And for the first time Nicola had recognised her own mistakes in the relationship. She'd bottled up all her resentment and pain and had never told her mother how she'd really felt. But now...

Now they were taking it one day at a time. Relationships like theirs didn't heal overnight, but she had to give her mother credit for trying. Yes, she still occasionally nagged Nicola, but she'd also become incredibly supportive.

Cade had been right—we did teach others how to treat us.

'Are you sure you're happy going to this wretched wedding? Nobody would blame you if you changed your mind, you know?'

'I'm fine, Mum, honestly. The truth is, Diane did me a favour.'

A fact confirmed the first time she'd clapped eyes on the couple when she'd returned to Melbourne. In fact, with Cade so fresh in her mind, Brad had seemed pale and lacking in dynamism...a touch inadequate even. She couldn't believe she'd almost married him.

At the thought of Cade, a cloud drifted across the brightness of the day. Unlike Brad, his influence had not waned with time.

'You know, Nicola Ann, I'm not sure I ever really did like Brad.'

She had to smile at that.

'But I still don't like what Diane did. She was supposed to be your friend.'

'I guess these things happen, Mum.'

She'd accepted that her friendship with Diane had irrevocably changed. There were days she missed their old closeness, but she also enjoyed a new sense of freedom and independence. She'd joined a riding club and she'd started taking singing lessons. She enjoyed her work at the primary school.

But none of it had been able to drive Cade from her mind. None of it had lessened her yearning for him. Without fail, every week she and Ella had a Skype session. But not once had Cade popped his head into view to say hello and ask her how she was doing. And yet, every week she kept her fingers crossed that he would.

She'd tried her best to get over him. She'd had three dates since she'd returned home. Two had ended in a goodnight kiss at the front door. There hadn't been a single spark or flutter or firework. After her last date she'd had to accept what had been staring her in the face for four long months—she'd fallen in love with Cade. She'd fallen in love with him properly, truly and without agenda.

'So why do you look as if the sky is about to fall in?'

She shook herself. She was about to lie and say nothing was the matter, but she knew her mother would see through the lie and be hurt by it. Their newfound understanding was too new to risk damaging with casual deceit. 'That has nothing to do with Diane or Brad.'

'I know,' Angela said softly. 'You only started looking like that once you returned from that cattle station of yours.'

Her mother had noticed? Tears pricked the back of her eyes. 'I'm fine, Mum.'

'I know, but I can't help worrying about you.'

The doorbell rang.

'That'll be your cab. Put on your shoes and powder your nose one last time while I answer the door.'

Nicola did as her mother bid. She stared in the mirror,

pressed the powder puff to her nose…then she put it away and hitched up her chin. Falling in love with Cade was unfortunate, yes, but not insurmountable. At least, she hoped not. Eventually his memory would fade. When it did she would date again. One thing was for sure, though—she didn't regret turning down his offer of marriage. Not for a moment. Not even in a weak moment.

She collected her clutch and wrap and with a deep breath headed for the living room.

'Nicola, this gentleman says he knows you. He claims he's your date for the evening.'

Nicola glanced up as she walked into the living room, to find Cade's bulk framed in the doorway. Wind rushed past her ears, drowning out the rest of her mother's words. She reached out a hand to steady herself on the back of a chair. Cade stood there—*in her living room in Melbourne*—dressed in a tuxedo, and all she could do was stare…and stare…and stare some more. She blinked but he didn't disappear. She gripped the back of the chair more tightly to prevent herself from doing something stupid like racing over to him and hurling herself into his arms.

He shrugged. He didn't smile. 'We had a deal. Did you think I'd forget?'

Cade suspected he might be about to make the biggest fool of himself, but he wasn't sure he cared. Not when it meant seeing Nicola in the flesh and drawing her unique strawberry jam scent into his lungs. He stared at her and something inside him that had stopped and seized the day her plane had taken off from Waminda, started to unfurl, to relax…to tick with anticipation.

He ached to take the three strides that would bring him right up against her, wrap an arm around her waist and pull her hard up against him and kiss her until neither one of them could think.

But she deserved a whole lot more finesse than that. Besides, it might help slake the need pounding through him, but it was her need that counted.

She stared at him with those amazing eyes, but she didn't smile. Her tongue snaked out to moisten her lips. 'I…um…'

She had! She'd thought he'd forgotten their deal. It took an effort of will not to rock back on his heels. He resisted the urge to run a finger around the collar of his shirt as it tightened about his throat. 'Did you organise another date?' His voice scraped out of his throat, but he couldn't help it, couldn't modulate it. He tried to swallow.

Was someone else taking his Cinderella to the ball? His hands clenched about the bunch of flowers he held. He wasn't sure what he'd do if she said yes.

The older woman who'd answered the door nudged Nicola. 'Darling?'

Nicola jumped. Colour flooded her cheeks. 'I really didn't think you'd… I mean, I never really thought that you were serious.'

Of course she hadn't. She thought him a lowlife—the kind of man who'd propose a loveless marriage. He *had* done that and it *did* make him a lowlife. His hands clenched tightly. If he was lucky he might be able to redeem himself a little this evening. The stems of the flowers dug into his hands.

'You…' Her voice trembled. She swallowed. 'You never mentioned it again.'

'I always keep my word.'

'How…' Her tongue moistened her lips and need clenched through him. 'How did you know when it was on?'

'You told Ella. You showed her your dress.' He wondered if he would ever be able to unclench his hand from around the flowers. 'In one of your Skype sessions. I listened in to them all.'

'You never once said hello.'

He could see now what a mistake that had been.

Her hands twisted together. 'I wish you hadn't gone to so much trouble.'

It was all he could do to keep his voice steady. 'No trouble at all.' *She was going to shaft him!* She was going to tell him she had another date, and that he'd wasted his time. She was going to tell him to go home.

With every second that passed the atmosphere grew tenser. The older woman stepped forward to take the flowers. Probably before he could strangle them completely. She had to almost prise them from his hand. She glanced at Nicola and cleared her throat delicately.

Nicola jumped again. 'Mum, this is Cade Hindmarsh, the owner of Waminda Downs station where I was nanny during the Christmas break. Cade, this is my mother, Angela McGillroy.'

Nicola's mother? She was nothing like he'd imagined. He did his best not to stare. 'Pleased to meet you.'

'Charmed,' she returned but her eyes narrowed. 'Do you want to attend the wedding with this man, Nicola, or would you like me to send him packing?'

He might be twice her size but he didn't doubt her ability to dispatch him with ruthless efficiency if she so chose.

He raised an eyebrow. 'Nicola?' If she'd truly prefer to attend the wedding on her own, or if she had another date, he'd leave. He planted his feet and lifted his chin. But he'd be back here first thing tomorrow morning. They had to talk.

His lips twisted. No, correction—he had to beg. His

gut tightened. Hopefully, Nicola would listen. It'd be more than he deserved, he knew that, but he had to give it a go.

Still, scowling and pressing her weren't fair. He made himself smile and for a moment that wasn't hard because it was so damn good to see her. 'It's great to see you, Nicola. You look…fabulous.' He hoped his eyes conveyed just how fabulous he found her. 'And if you don't have another date I would be honoured to attend the wedding with you.'

She smiled back and just like that the ground beneath his feet shifted. 'Thank you, Cade, that would be lovely.'

The tightness in his chest eased when he realised he'd just won round one. As he led her to his hired car he reminded himself that this evening was about her. He meant to make this night special for her, his own impatience be damned. It was the least he could do. Nicola deserved the best and tonight he meant to give that to her. Or die trying.

Only then would he have the right to ask for her hand in marriage. And if he made it that far, this time he had every intention of doing it right.

For Cade, nothing was too much trouble. He anticipated Nicola's every want, he charmed her friends and he made all the right comments about the bride's dress, the brides-maids, the speeches and the food served at the reception. He even kept his thoughts about the bridegroom to himself. Though, hell… His lip curled. Nicola could do a hundred times better than that colourless prat.

She can do a hundred times better than you too.

Nicola smiled and chatted. She sighed her way through the service before asking if they could give another cou-ple a ride to the reception. She seemed to genuinely enjoy herself and none of that enjoyment seemed forced. The service and the reception didn't appear to give her pain or make her feel awkward. He kept an eagle eye out for either, ready to do whatever he could to help, to boost her confidence, but...

She didn't need it.

Her grace and poise impressed him. It also made him feel at a loss. He knew exactly how to fluster her. All it would take would be a sly caress to her arm and a scorching survey of her lips and—

This is about her, not you!

He refreshed her glass of champagne and, for what felt like the first time that evening, found himself alone with her. 'Is it the ordeal you thought it would be?'

She sipped her champagne and then shook her head. 'No, it's been kind of nice and a lot of fun.'

She hadn't needed him at all. His heart burned at that realisation. 'Would you like to dance?'

Slowly she shook her head. 'I think I'd rather just chat.'

He ached to hold her in his arms, but wasn't sure of his own strength on that score. He gritted his teeth. Chatting would be good. He held her chair out for her. She sat and he planted himself in the seat beside her. 'Your mother isn't anything like I imagined.'

Her eyes lit up and she leaned towards him, swamping him with the sweetness of her scent. 'We had the most amazing discussion when I got home from Waminda.'

'Tell me,' he urged.

They talked for three straight hours. Cade couldn't believe it was time to take her home.

He tucked her into the car and then slid in behind the wheel. 'The night is yet young. Would you like to go to a bar or a club? We could go for a drink or go dancing or—'

'Why?'

The single question pulled him to a halt. He met her gaze. His heart pounded. 'There's quite a long answer to that.'

She stared at him for several long moments and he didn't kid himself that the outcome of those moments would not seal his fate. They would. He held his breath while his chest cramped.

'A walk along the Southbank would be nice. We could grab a coffee, maybe.'

He lifted her hand from her lap and brushed his lips across the backs of her fingers. 'Thank you.'

Nicola's heart thudded against her ribs as she and Cade walked beside the river, the Southbank foreshore bright with lights, Saturday night revelry and Melbourne's bright young things. It was vibrant, zesty and normally she loved it.

Tonight, though, she couldn't focus on it. Tonight, all her attention was on the man who walked beside her with a stern expression on his face and a contrasting warmth in his eyes. He didn't try to take her hand or touch her in any way. She did all she could to combat a growing sense of disappointment.

It was for the best. She knew it was for the best. Her body, however, refused to believe it, found no consolation in common sense.

And, God forgive her, but she couldn't help but lap up every exquisite minute she spent in his company. She closed her eyes and savoured the sound of his voice. She drank in the familiar way he held his head, the breadth of his shoulders and the long masculine stride he adjusted to her shorter ones. The smiles he sent her.

And the warmth in his eyes.

She stowed them all away deep in her heart to take out and cherish later, because she didn't fool herself. Tomorrow he would be gone and in all likelihood she would never see him again. The thought made her heartbeat pound in her ears and pain throb in her chest. She pushed it away. Tomorrow—she'd deal with it tomorrow.

She didn't urge him to talk. The sooner he'd said whatever it was he needed to say, the sooner he'd take her home and this strange, exhilarating, bittersweet night would end. She didn't take his arm and lead him into one of the restaurants or cafés that lined the riverside either. She didn't want to share him with the crowds, the light or the laughter.

Her heart gave a giant surge when he took her hand and led her to a bench that overlooked the river. For a moment she thought he was going to keep a hold of her, but then he let go.

She sat and stared out at the river to hide her disappointment. Those blue eyes of his had always seen too much.

'There's a lot I want to say, Nicola.'

She counted to three and when she was sure of herself, she looked up. She wished her eyes were half as perceptive as his. She'd give anything to know what he was thinking. She remembered the way he'd held her when she'd cried, the way he'd fed her chocolate sultanas and the way they'd laughed and laughed on the veranda that night, and she nodded. 'We have all night, Cade. There's nowhere else I need to be.'

'Good.' He nodded, and then sat. He rested his elbows on his knees, hands lightly clasped in front of him and lips pursed as he stared out at the dark river. Then he straightened again and met her gaze. 'First, I want to apologise to you for that appalling proposal of marriage. I didn't see at the time what an insult it was. I do now and I want you to know I am truly and deeply sorry.'

'That's okay.' It was an automatic response, but she didn't doubt his sincerity.

'It wasn't okay.' He shook his head, but then his lips tilted a fraction. 'That said, I'm still hoping you'll forgive me.' His eyes glittered in the half dark. 'You deserve so much more than that half-baked scheme I offered. You deserve a man who worships the very ground you walk on.'

Her breath caught at the force of his words. And then her heart started to burn. Cade was never going to be that man, was he?

She swallowed back a lump. 'I accept your apology, Cade. All's forgiven. You panicked, that's all.'

She suddenly wanted away from here, away from this man who would never love her the way she wanted him to love her. The sweetness of their meeting could no longer counter its bitterness. She shot to her feet, but then didn't know what to do. She took a couple of steps forward to stare down at the water.

'I've missed you, Nicola.'

She dragged in a breath. She folded her arms and turned back. 'I've missed all of you too.'

His eyes didn't waver as he rose and joined her. 'Yes— Ella, Holly, Harry and Jack all miss you as well. But I'm not talking about them. I'm talking about me. *I* miss you.'

Her mouth went dry. She couldn't speak.

'And yes, I miss seeing you with the girls. I miss watching you tickle Holly until she's laughing uncontrollably, and I miss the way you and Ella have the most serious conversations and then Ella jumps up smiling as if you've given her the secret of the universe. I'd be lying if I said I didn't miss those things. They're not what I miss the most, though.'

They weren't? Her heartbeat drummed out a tattoo she thought anyone within a ten-metre radius must hear.

'I miss the scent of strawberry jam in my days. I miss watching you walk across a room where I can admire the very shape of you.'

Heat flared in her cheeks.

'I miss the shape of your mouth. I miss the taste of you.'

'Oh!' She pressed her hands to her cheeks in an effort to cool them.

He shrugged and sent her a sheepish grin. 'What can I say? I'm a guy. It's how I'm wired.' He took her hands. 'But even those aren't the things I miss the most. I miss...' He stilled. 'I miss talking with you—proper, honest talking with no game playing. I miss laughing with you until my sides hurt. I miss someone noticing the minute I walk into a room.'

His hands tightened around hers. 'I miss someone sensing when something is troubling me. I miss sensing that about you. I miss your laugh. I miss the way you eye chocolate sultanas as if they're the devil's own food and the way you eat them as if they're manna from heaven. I miss the way you lift your face to the sky when you're cantering on Scarlett. I miss the way you stare up at a night sky as if it's the most magical thing you've ever seen. More than anything, I miss your smile. I *really* miss your smile.'

She stared at him. She couldn't say a word as she tried to process his words and what they meant. He missed her, but that didn't mean...

He led her back to the bench. She collapsed onto it, her shaky knees grateful for the respite. Cade didn't sit. He paced up and down in front of her.

'It took me a long time to find an answer to your question.'

'Which one?' she croaked.

'The one about Fran...and what I'd do if she came back and wanted to start over.'

She leaned back although every atom of her being strained towards him. 'And?'

'I'd welcome her back into the girls' lives because she's their mother.'

Nicola nodded. That had always gone without saying.

He frowned and paced harder. 'And then I got all caught up on whether I would choose Fran for the girls—Fran, who has proven herself unreliable—or a woman who I trusted and respected and who I believed wouldn't let the girls down.'

'And?'

'And then I realised that was wrong thinking. I'd welcome Fran back into Ella and Holly's lives.' He stopped pacing. He stopped right in front of her. 'But I wouldn't welcome her back into my life. You were right, Nicola, when you said you deserved better than what I'd offered, that you deserved love and friendship. It hit me then that I deserved those things too. And they're not something I can ever find with Fran.'

Her jaw dropped. Her heart thumped. He looked as if... as if... 'I didn't think you believed in love any more—a fairy tale, isn't that what you called it?'

'It's what I wanted to believe—to protect myself from being hurt again.' He drew her to her feet. 'But then a no-nonsense nanny with killer curves and a smile that practically knocked me off my feet swept into my life and made me feel alive again...made me feel things I never had before and I...'

A smile started up in the depths of her. 'Panicked?' she offered.

He cupped her face. 'Nicola, I have absolutely no right to expect you to believe me, but I love you.'

She wanted to believe him—so much it hurt. The light in his eyes as they rested on her lips left her in no doubt whatsoever that he desired her.

'When Fran left, my life went into a tailspin of shock, panic and pain at the trauma the girls suffered. When you left, it felt as if I'd lost a limb, as if nothing in me worked properly any more.'

Her heart lurched and then thumped hard and fast. What he'd described fitted her own state during these last few months so perfectly that suddenly she knew he spoke the truth. He wasn't after a mother for his children, but a wife to share his life.

He loved her!

He went down on one knee. 'Nicola, I can offer you a family who will adore you, friendship, a horse, life on an Outback station—and if any of those things will sway you I'll use them shamelessly—but mostly I can offer you a heart filled with love for you. I love you, my beautiful girl. I will love you till the day I die. Please say that you'll marry me and let me spend the rest of my life proving to you just how much I do love you.'

Her heart had grown so big she thought she might explode. She knelt down on the ground in front of him and took his face in her hands. She smiled at him with her whole heart. He blinked…and she watched as hope stretched across his face. 'Can we get rid of that awful home gym?'

'Consider it gone.' He grinned that lazy, tempting grin that never failed to bump up her heart rate. 'And I promise to always keep the cupboards stocked with chocolate sultanas.'

Her heart pounded. She leaned forward and pressed her lips to his. For a moment he seemed too stunned to respond but, just as she was about to draw back, his arms flashed around her and he held her so tightly she could barely breathe. He kissed her so thoroughly her head swam and she had to cling to him for support.

He lifted his head. 'I love you, Nicola. I can't even begin to describe how much.'

Her breath hitched. 'I don't know. I think you did a pretty good job.' She reached out to touch his face. 'My days have all been grey these last four months. I missed you so much. I didn't want to believe I'd fallen in love with you—I thought it would prove that I was needy and weak.'

He frowned. 'Do you still believe that?'

She shook her head. 'I know that if you ever walked away from me that I'd survive, but…oh, how much better my life is with you in it!'

Determination blazed in his eyes. 'Are you going to marry me?'

She smiled. She grinned. She threw her head back and laughed. 'Yes!'

He stared at her as if she was the most magnificent thing he had ever seen. 'When can I take you home to Waminda?'

Home. The word stretched through her, full of promise. Wherever this man was, that would be her home. And she would be his.

'Just as soon as we give my mother the wedding she's always dreamed of,' she breathed.

'Whatever will make you happy,' he swore.

And she knew he meant it.

* * * * *